FOR BETTER AND

Whenever Darcy had
always the groom in the fantasy. But an *older* Stan, starting up his own architectural firm. She was older in the fantasy too – self-possessed and sophisticated, a reporter for a major newspaper, on call for fast-breaking stories all over the world. They'd come back to Kenosha for the wedding so their families could be there, so Darcy could walk down the aisle of the beautiful church on a sunny day in June in her grandmother's heirloom lace-and-satin gown.

Her *actual* wedding day turned out quite a bit differently . . .

MAYBE BABY

A novel by Carol Stanley

Based on a screenplay by
Tim Kazurinsky & Denise DeClue

CORGI AVON

MAYBE BABY
A CORGI/AVON BOOK 0 552 13432 5

Published by arrangement with Avon Books, 105 Madison Avenue, New York 10016

First publication in Great Britain

PRINTING HISTORY

Corgi/Avon edition published 1988

Published by arrangement with Tri-Star Pictures, Inc.

Corgi Books are published by Transworld Publishers Ltd., 61-63 Uxbridge Road, Ealing, London W5 5SA, in Australia by Transworld Publishers (Australia) Pty. Ltd., 15-23 Helles Avenue, Moorebank, NSW 2170, and in New Zealand by Transworld Publishers (N.Z.) Ltd., Cnr. Moselle and Waipareira Avenues, Henderson, Auckland.

Reproduced, printed and bound in Great Britain by
Hazell Watson & Viney Limited
Member of BPCC plc
Aylesbury, Bucks, England

Chapter 1

"Darcy, darling! *Ma chère!* Time to get up!"

"Argh," Darcy moaned, opening one eye, quickly shutting it, and pulling her pillow over her head. A personal version of the snooze alarm. This usually bought her five more minutes' freedom from her mother's cheerfulness. The two of them were total morning opposites. Darcy's own mood when she woke up was about that of an annoyed alligator. Especially this summer when, most days, she had to go to her hated summer job—running the dishwasher at the Paul Bunyan House of Flapjacks. She was sure she'd never be able to even *look* at blueberry syrup again as long as she lived.

But now, in the utter darkness under her pillow, her eyes popped open as she realized that she didn't have to hide out this morning. She didn't have anything to avoid. Today was Saturday. The last Saturday of August. The day she was going up to Madison to check out the University of Wisconsin.

She sat up like a jack-in-the-box.

"All *right!*" she said as she jumped out of bed, grabbed fresh underwear and jeans and her best 1950s retro shirt, and headed for the shower. Darcy prided herself on being the fastest person alive in the getting-ready department. She could shower in a couple of minutes, dress in less. And aside from blowing her long hair dry, she hardly spent a second in front of a mirror. By the time she was thirteen, she'd pretty much figured out the basics about her looks—that her long red hair had a will of its own, that she should *never* wear purple lipstick, and that although she wasn't a classic beauty, she did have a certain off-center style.

As she came downstairs, she could smell the cinnamon her mother always put in their coffee—"the continental touch," Mrs. Elliot called it.

"Do you want some breakfast?" her mother called out from the kitchen.

"Just coffee," Darcy said, pouring a cup before heading into the dining room. "I've got to finish this article."

She sat down at the table in front of her old beat-up electric typewriter and tried to come up with the brilliant concluding paragraph that had eluded her last night. She began tapping away at the keys and was soon so absorbed that she didn't even hear the doorbell ring.

"Darcy! Lila's here! *Allons-y. On y va! Vite! Vite!"* Darcy heard her mother bustling through the living room to the front door.

"Hi, Mrs. Elliot."

"Bonjour, Lila. Comment ca va?"

Darcy knew that her mother liked Lila—partly because she thought she was smart and well behaved, partly because she thought it was sophisticated that Darcy's best friend was black. Darcy's mother was big on sophistication.

Lila came into the living room and gave Darcy a "hurry up" look.

"Almost done," Darcy told her.

Lila came around behind her and looked over Darcy's shoulder. "Isn't that your article on the senator's campaign?"

"Mmmhmm," Darcy murmured, her attention absorbed by the words in front of her.

"This campus preview weekend will be such an enriching experience for you girls," Darcy's mother was saying. "Two days at a real college. I know Darcy would love for me to come, but I have to work if she and I are going to do Paris in style."

"That's what Darcy told me," Lila said politely, then, turning to Darcy, "I thought you filed that story yesterday."

"I was going to, but his press conference last night changed everything." Darcy was a perfectionist as a reporter, a stickler on getting all the facts—even if it pushed her hard against a deadline. She was on the last sentence when the typewriter jammed, machine-gunning one letter across the whole page.

"Damn! I hate this stupid machine!" she said, opening her bottle of white-out and dabbing the error away. She didn't bother waiting for the page to dry, just yanked it out of the typewriter and stuffed it into the briefcase sitting on the chair next to her.

"There!" she said. "Finished. I'll mail this on the road." She grabbed her nylon backpack, took Lila by the elbow, and started pulling her out of the living room—all in one long series of movements. She wanted to get out of the house before her mother really got on a roll of questions.

"So, you'll be staying overnight in a dorm?" her mother asked; catching up with them at the front door, where she stood practically nose to nose with Darcy. "Not that I'm prying," Mrs. Elliot went on. "You're entitled to your space, of course."

"Mom," Darcy said, "you're *standing* in my space."

Outside the house, her mother stood on the front

steps and called lightly. "Be careful of those university men!"

"Right, Mother," Darcy called back over her shoulder. "I'm sure they'll all be naked."

"Go ahead. Make fun . . . Actually, I was thinking it would be nice if there *were* boys—*new* boys. There, I've said it. Go. *Au revoir.*"

Darcy and Lila exchanged a Significant Look as they got to Lila's old beat-up VW. They both had to climb in on the passenger side. The driver-side door handle had been broken off since forever. Lila started the car up while Darcy tossed her bags into the back seat. Over the sputter of the engine, the girls heard Mrs. Elliot calling out from the front porch, "Lila! You drive carefully!"

Lila slapped her forehead and said to Darcy, "Great idea. Why didn't *I* think of that?"

To Mrs. Elliot, though, she just waved cheerfully out of the window and smiled. As they were driving off, she shook her head and said to Darcy, "Your mother . . ."

"I know. Too cool for Kenosha. She really belongs in Paris."

As they drove down Willow Street, Darcy turned around and looked out the window. She could see her mother still standing on the porch, watching them leave. When the VW finally turned the corner onto Morningside Drive, Darcy let out a huge sigh of relief.

"Boy, I thought I'd never get out of there. I'm so *nervous*. Did it show, do you think? What time is it, anyway?" She lifted Lila's hand off the gearshift and turned her wrist so she could read her watch. "Seven-twelve. Well, I don't suppose he'll leave me behind for being twelve minutes late."

Lila groaned.

"Seven A.M. on a Saturday, and where am I? Deep in slumberland? Noooo. I'm up at dawn so I can take my best friend on a one-block drive. Honey, you really owe me one—a *major* one. Like if we're ever stranded out in the middle of the Sahara desert, and there's only enough water for one of us in the canteen . . ."

"It's all yours, Lila. Every drop. Really. I am hugely, eternally appreciative of this favor." Darcy stopped suddenly, as if she'd had the breath suddenly taken out of her. "Oh," she said.

Lila wondered what had stopped her in midsentence. Then she saw. Stan's Volvo was parked in the middle of the block. He was leaning against it, his arms crossed in front of him as he watched them approach. Or rather watched Darcy approach. Stan was so in love that when Darcy was around, he usually couldn't focus on anything else.

Lila pulled up behind the Volvo. Stan came over and poked his head into the car.

"Hi, Lila. Mind if I take off with my girl?"

Darcy gave Lila a hug, then grabbed her backpack and hopped out of the VW. She gave Stan a long kiss, then stood back for a moment. It was amazing to her how, after going with him since junior high, sometimes just seeing him after being apart for a day or night could still give her this funny rush.

"This *is* pretty romantic," Lila mused as she put Darcy's briefcase in the back seat of the Volvo. "You two going off together. Alone, together, for the first time. Spending the night. Together."

Meanwhile Stan and Darcy were checking out the car.

"You got the map?" Stan asked Darcy.

She fumbled around in the glove compartment and found it. "Map," she said. "Tapes?"

"Tapes," Stan said, pulling the carrying case out from under the seat. "Thermos?"

Darcy picked up what she thought was the thermos and said, "Full."

"That's the flashlight," Stan informed her as they got into the car.

Darcy stuck her head out the window and looked at Lila, who looked around and then up at the sky, wincing. "Is it always this light this early?" She was working afternoons at McDonald's for the summer and usually slept until about noon. She even had aluminum foil over her windows to keep the sun out.

"Thanks for covering," Darcy told her.

As Stan started up the Volvo, Lila was saying dreamily, "Bye. I wish Ron and I could go off . . . alone . . . together."

"How'd it go with your mother?" Stan asked Darcy when they had turned onto the highway.

"Easy as pie," Darcy said. "I wonder if they really *do* have a campus preview weekend? What'd you end up telling your folks?"

"I'm camping with Chris."

Darcy had to laugh. "Oh, boy," she said, thinking of the web of lies they were tangling themselves up in. "If we get caught, are we ever going to be in *deep* trouble."

Stan looked at Darcy, smiled his slow smile, and said, "Yeah, but if we don't, are we ever going to have a great time!"

He put the Volvo in gear and peeled out, and together they shouted out the windows, "Whhhaaaa-hoooo!"

Chapter 2

Stan wanted to take the old highway up to Madison. "So we can really *see* the countryside." So they wound their way in the old Volvo through tiny towns, past miles and miles of farm fields and grazing land.

"Look at those sheep!" Darcy said, pointing. "All in a clump, all eating at the same time."

"Why, those sheep are just like *sheep!*" Stan said in mock surprise, making Darcy laugh.

"Oh, look!" Darcy said a few miles later, reading a road sign, *"Wisconsin Cheese Specialties Just Ahead.* Can we stop for some cheese specialties?" She reached over and tickled him around the ribs. "Can we, huh? A little cheese snack-o for the weary travelers?"

"But, honey, we've only been on the road for half an hour," Stan moaned. Then he looked over at Darcy, who was turned toward him, her hands folded in praying position. "Oh, all right!" he said, grinning in defeat.

A few minutes later, Darcy was standing at the checkout counter inside the International House of Cheese attached to the Mobil station on the highway. The cashier was tallying up Darcy's purchases.

"That's one cheddar-nut log, two baby Edams, and a gouda humor bar."

Darcy didn't hear a word of this. Her total attention was focused like a laser through the front window of the store. The cashier, a girl close to Darcy's age, looked out to see what could be so fascinating about a cluster of gas pumps. Then she too saw Stan, who was goofing off, playing a one-man game of basketball with a wadded-up towel and garbage drum.

"That your boyfriend?" the cashier asked.

"Mmmhmm. Five years," Darcy said.

"Cute."

"Thanks," Darcy said, then added, "Smart, too." She thought of adding a few more of his qualities. She could tell this girl about the way his eyes sort of crinkled around the edges when he laughed. And how he still sometimes showed up for a date with flowers in hand, even though it was terribly corny. And how at the end of school last year, he'd stayed up all night with her to teach her practically all of geometry the night before the final. And how, even though he was a guy, she could still talk to him about stuff other girls only talked to their girlfriends about—traumatic haircuts, getting snubbed by someone.

But then Darcy thought better. She didn't want to sound like one of those girls who are goony about their boyfriends—even though she probably was.

On the highway again, Stan asked, "How far to Madison from here?"

Darcy looked down at the map opened on her lap. "About another hour," she said. "If . . . you know . . . we don't stop."

"What if we do . . . you know . . . stop?" Stan asked.

"We might never get there," Darcy said.

So they kept on going until they got to Madison. By the time they passed the University of Wisconsin sign, it was almost noon. The campus had a sleepy summer look to it. Sprinklers were whooshing over wide green lawns; bees were idly buzzing in the flowers around the classroom and dorm buildings. Darcy and Stan wandered hand in hand, taking it all in.

"Is this a beautiful campus, or what?" Darcy said. She had wanted to come here ever since she found out how good their journalism school was, but she hadn't known it would also be so beautiful, or so big. "It's so . . . so . . . collegiate," she said, sighing.

Stan looked around at the students on their way to summer classes, or playing Frisbee, or just hanging out, lying around on the grass talking with one another.

"Everyone looks so happy," he said.

"Because their mothers are hundreds of miles away," Darcy said. Then, spotting what she was looking for, she gave Stan's hand a squeeze and dashed off. "There it is!"

By the time he caught up with her, she was already there, standing in front of the communications building, looking up at it in awe. She clutched to her chest the scrapbook of articles she'd written for her high school newspaper.

"They don't even let you into the journalism school till junior year. But if I get this internship . . ." She crossed her fingers and tapped Stan on the nose.

"You mean *when* you get this internship . . ." he corrected her.

"I'll be their star reporter!" Darcy said.

"Then you'll get your own column!" Stan said.

"Then I'll be the editor!" Darcy said, laughing as Stan ran up the front steps of the building, turned around and around, and then loudly proclaimed, "And then Darcy Elliot won the Pulitzer Prize. And they named this building after her."

"The Her Building!" Darcy shouted. Then, weak

from laughing, she rushed up the steps and dragged Stan off to the student union before any more people stopped to stare.

Darcy was supposed to meet Markus Sloane and Beth Harris—the coeditors of the college paper—at noon. She was hoping they'd be real down-to-earth, casual, easygoing types, but as soon as she walked into the union and saw a skinny, intense couple furiously smoking and drinking coffee and marking up galleys on a couch in the back, she knew it had to be them. Stan nodded that she should go over alone.

"I'll just hang out. Look at the old football stuff on the walls here. You know. This is *your* thing."

"I know," Darcy said. "I want to do it alone."

Ten minutes later, Darcy was sitting on the couch, fanning away cigarette smoke, dying with nervousness while Markus and Beth looked through her book of clips. Finally Markus said, in a voice dripping with sarcasm, "Fascinating. You mean your state representative *actually* spoke at your school assembly? Stop the presses."

"Did you read what he said?" Darcy asked, proud of her story. "He really gave it to our mayor."

"Oh, this is cute," Beth said, looking at another page. "'Swampy Soccer Field Flooded With Frogs.'"

"There were a couple of thousand of them," Darcy said defensively. "I checked with the Department of Agriculture and . . ."

Markus and Beth exchanged a look.

"Quite a story. Hope the *Washington Post* picked it up."

"Look, Farkus," Darcy said. "I'm sure this is all small potatoes to you . . ."

"Markus . . ."

Darcy snatched her scrapbook, got up from the couch, glared at him, and kept right on talking.

". . . but those frogs happened to be big news at my school. And big news in Kenosha—which is where I live, and where I find my stories. Kenosha is my beat, and I try to cover it *in depth*. And if you'd taken the time to read my stories instead of just making fun of the headlines, you might have seen . . ."

He looked at her wide-eyed, clearly at least a little impressed.

"Tell you what," he said. "Send me what you write this year for your paper. Let's see what we can do. I like your passion."

Stan, who had been walking over to see what was going on, stopped a few feet away from Darcy and broke into a wide smile.

"She's good, isn't she?" he said, his voice filled with pride.

"You going to school here, too?" Markus asked him.

Stan shook his head. "Cal Tech. Architecture. *If* my scholarship comes through."

Darcy rumpled Stan's hair and told Markus and Beth. "He'll get it."

"So he'll be in California . . . and you'll be here," Beth said.

"We'll pull it off," Darcy told her.

"Live for holidays and vacations, right?" Markus said.

Put that way, it didn't sound too terrific, but Stan jumped in with bravado. "Sure," he told them, and Darcy backed him up.

"Definitely!" she said, but then she looked at Stan and saw him looking back at her with the same stuff in his eyes. They were missing each other already. Until now, it hadn't hit her just how hard it was going to be, being apart. Being without Stan in her everydays, making their lives a long, running story they were creating together.

By dusk, Darcy and Stan had found a beautiful place in a woods outside of Madison, eaten their wilderness campsite dinner—Big Macs, fries, and shakes—and were working hard at putting up their tent before night fell.

It was the first time the tent had ever been put up. Stan had designed it for them. They put in the center poles, sunk the stakes, and tied up the guy lines, then stood back to look at their masterpiece.

"Oh, Stan!" Darcy raved. "It's fantastic! It looks exactly like your design—*exactly!*"

"Well, my mom really did all the hard work, all the sewing."

Darcy kissed him and pulled him into a slow dance around the campsite, moving to a new Pretenders song playing on the radio propped on a rock, their bodies casting strange shadows in the light of the campfire.

Darcy opened the plaid thermos they'd filled with wine. She filled the plastic cap half full and held it aloft in a toast.

"Here's to forever," she said.

"To holidays," Stan said as she sipped, mocking the college paper editor.

"And vacations," Darcy said, passing the cup to Stan.

They wrapped their arms around each other and continued to dance, real slow.

"I don't know," Darcy said. "People *can* drift apart. Things happen."

"That's right," Stan said, his mouth next to her ear.

"Things *happen*. *I* happen . . . to be . . . in love with you."

They kissed a long kiss—but not quite as long as it would have been if Darcy hadn't opened her eyes and taken a closer look at the tent.

"Oh, wow!" she shouted, jumping back. "A skylight! You put in a skylight!"

She pulled him over to the tent.

"You are unbelievable," she told him. "Someday you are going to knock the architectural world on its ear!"

As Darcy pulled back the tent flap and started inside, Stan pulled her back for a moment and said, "You like the skylight? Wait till I show you the sauna."

By dawn, it was as though the weather had pulled itself inside out. After a night of kissing and holding each other and talking and watching the starlit skies through the Plexiglas roof of the tent, this morning they were facing a raging storm, with rain whipping around them in sheets as they tried to dismantle the tent. And on top of it all, they'd overslept and were already late.

"I set the alarm," Darcy moaned. "I just forgot to pull out the little thing on the back of the clock."

"It's okay," Stan said, trying to calm her down. But she just got more agitated.

"If I'm late and my mother starts calling over to Lila's . . ."

Stan grabbed her and looked her hard in the eyes. "We're not going to be late," he said, then got an impish grin on his face. "We'll just skip breakfast."

"We'll still be a little late," Darcy said, pulling herself close to him, kissing him, letting him kiss her, then adding, "Well, I guess a *little* late couldn't hurt."

They sank to the ground together, onto the collapsed tent, overwhelmed by what they were feeling for each other, their own private storm in the midst of the one raging around them.

Chapter 3

Darcy followed Stan through the cafeteria line, pushing her tray behind his. "Here, have a pear. Good for you." She picked one out of the fruit bowl at the end of the line and set it on his tray.

"Guy can't even pick his own lunch," Stan groused, although both he and Darcy knew he liked the attention.

Lila swept by with a couple of girls from her American history class. "Missed you in gym," she called out to Darcy.

"Yeah, well I wasn't feeling . . ." Darcy let the sentence trail off vaguely. She wondered if she looked as crummy as she felt. She doubly wondered it when Michaela slid her tray in front of Stan's. Michaela looked terrific—in a vampy way. Just the way you didn't want someone to look if she was putting a big piece of chocolate pie on your boyfriend's tray—which was what was happening at this very moment.

"You need something sweet in your diet," she said in a voice that was really more a purr. Michaela was clearly after Stan, a fact that had been slowly dawning on Darcy for a couple of weeks. She didn't have time to deal with it right now, though. She saw a more immediate target of her attention across the lunch room.

"Yikes! There's Mrs. Fanelli. She's been ducking me all morning. I've got to interview her for the paper." She grabbed a pen out of Stan's shirt pocket and dashed into the kitchen.

"Go get her," Stan said. "I'll take your tray."

"And I'll see that he eats properly," Michaela cooed.

Darcy gave her a look that said, "I *bet* you will."

On her way back to the kitchen, Darcy pulled out her notepad and slipped on her glasses, transforming herself into Darcy Elliot, Girl Reporter. Ordinarily, there was nothing that got her revved up like a tough interview. Today, though, she didn't even really feel like doing this. She just wanted to go home and take a nice long nap. But—in the spirit of Woodward and Bernstein—she knew the presses had to roll, so she took a couple of deep breaths and held up her pencil.

"Oh, Mrs. Fanelli—I've been trying to call you."

Mrs. Fanelli, the school dietitian, had been busily heading for the stoves, but she turned and flashed Darcy her friendliest smile. Clearly she knew this was for the school paper and was putting on her best face.

"Been busy, Darcy. Working on a new rice pudding recipe."

"I understand a student verified an actual fingernail in a baked apple last week," Darcy said, in her best Ted Koppel manner.

But Mrs. Fanelli had nerves of steel. She just called Darcy's bluff, reaching for a large tray of little rice pudding cups and holding it out in front of Darcy.

"I want you to sample this personally," she said.

"Uh, no. Thanks, anyway," Darcy said, looking at the tray and suddenly feeling as if she were on a boat on a rice pudding sea. A wave of nausea coursed through her. She waited for it to pass, then started in on Mrs. Fanelli again.

"And I have it from a reliable source that a substitute teacher pulled a human hair from—"

Her friend Retro, who worked in the kitchen, overheard this and replied, "That's a vicious lie, Darcy . . . It wasn't human."

Darcy flicked the side of his head with her notepad, but then had to back away. Retro was dicing onions, and the smell slapped her in the face. She had to hold onto the counter for a moment to keep her balance.

"You're not answering my questions, Mrs. Fanelli," Darcy said weakly.

The dietitian took Darcy by the arm and led her over to the huge cafeteria stove.

"I'm not hiding anything, Darcy. Come. I want you to see the inner workings of this kitchen. This here is my latest culinary achievement—Chicken Fanelli!"

She lifted the lid off a giant, drum-sized vat, and Darcy peered inside. There were a dozen pale gray chickens floating in a yellowy liquid whose surface was slippery with fat globules. Darcy stared at this sight for a long moment, then suddenly put her hand to her mouth and ran out the back door of the kitchen.

Chapter 4

Darcy loved hanging out over at Stan's house. It was so different from her own home, where everything was "just so." Her mother's furniture was all French provincial, the color scheme coordinated. At Stan's, the "decor" consisted of a few recliner chairs and a couple of old color TVs. Where Darcy's mother had their walls hung with tasteful Impressionist prints, Mrs. Bobrucz—Stan's mother—had filled about every square inch of her wall space with photos of all the babies and graduations and weddings in the extremely extended Bobrucz family.

Dinner at Darcy's was always precisely at six and consisted of light, nutritiously planned meals. At Stan's, dinner was whenever his mother finished putting together one of her heavy but delicious Eastern European specialties—pierogi or goulash or potato soup. On nights when she wasn't up to cooking, dinner was whenever the pizza delivery guy arrived. Darcy was pretty sure her mother had never even eaten pizza. It just wasn't her style.

Sometimes Darcy was glad that her mother *had* all this style. Other times, she was relieved just to come over to Stan's and flop down on a sofa that no one minded if you put your feet up on.

This afternoon, she and Stan were studying together at his place, their feet up on the big old sprung sofa in the rec room. They were both taking chemistry this term and had a quiz the next day on the elements chart.

"Lead," he quizzed her.

"Pb," Darcy said.

"Hydrogen."

"H," she said. "I love hydrogen. It's so easy. Oxygen, too. They're my favorites. Want some gum?"

"What kind?"

Darcy stuck out her tongue and, on its tip, showed him the piece of gum she was chewing. He put an arm around her, gave her a kiss, took the gum, and popped it into his own mouth.

"Teenage romance," someone said from the doorway. It was Mary, Stan's eleven-year-old sister. "When you start to like boys—do you have to chew their gum?"

"Absolutely," Stan said.

"Absolutely," Darcy agreed. "But your brother's gum is the only other person's gum I've ever chewed."

"Is that what love is?" Mary asked thoughtfully.

Darcy thought for a second, then told Mary, "It's a start."

Mary—the original "inquiring mind"—gave all this information serious consideration, then suddenly reverted from her sophisticated preteen self to her last-days-of-childhood personality. She picked up a throw pillow from the chair next to the sofa and began making out with it.

"Oh, Darcy . . . Oh, Stan . . . Oh, Darcy," she said, mocking them.

Stan leapt off the sofa and, in one swift move, hoisted his sister over his head. "That's it! You're going out the window."

Mary, who was crazy about her big brother and

secretly loved being teased by him, wailed and moaned in fake terror. "No . . . no . . . no!"

"So what if we're in the basement? I'll still throw you out the window!" he said, carrying her aloft up into the kitchen, where his parents and his little brother Lou were just coming through the back door with the week's groceries.

Stan set Mary down and started poking around in the grocery bags, pulling out a package of cookies.

"Mom, Stan was going to throw me out the window."

"He was only kidding," Mrs. Bobrucz said, patting Mary on the head.

"No he wasn't," Stan said, handing a cookie to Darcy, who'd followed him into the kitchen, still trying to memorize her flash cards of the elements.

"Darcy?" Stan's mother said. "Stay for dinner? We're having gwumpkies."

"Then we're going to play a little minigolf," Mr. Bobrucz said, pulling a can of beer out of the refrigerator, popping the top with a giant fizz, and aiming it toward the sink.

"I'd love to, but I can't," Darcy said, a little embarrassed. "It's . . . well it's Thursday."

"French night," Lou reminded everybody.

"Ooo-la-la," Stan and his father teased in unison.

"Well, we got French fries right here," Stan's mother said.

"And French dressing!" Stan said, pulling a bottle out of one of the grocery bags that everyone was unpacking.

"French *toast,*" Stan's father added.

"Ice cream," Lou said. "French vanilla!"

"And French *kissing!*" Mary said, bursting into giggles at her own wit. "With gum . . ."

Her father turned and grabbed her up into the air with fake sternness.

"Hey, how do *you* know about that stuff?"

He growled ferociously and chased Mary out of the kitchen. Darcy leaned back against the refrigerator, trying to act insulted, but underneath loving this loony family. They were so high-energy, though sometimes it was exhausting being around all of them at once. Especially lately. For the past couple of weeks, Darcy had felt so *tired*. And not just in this madhouse. Twice this week she had fallen asleep in her sixth-period world history class. Maybe she was run down, or had some kind of virus. Or, then again, maybe it was Mr. Hopewell, who was an incredibly boring history teacher.

Promptly at six that night, Darcy and her mother sat down to their French dinner. Not only did they have French food, but they used these dinners to practice their French. Darcy had taken two years of it in school so far, and her mother was in a night course at the junior college. All of this was in preparation for the trip to Paris they were going to take together. Her mother's big dream. She'd been saving up for it for years now.

Darcy knew that a lot of people thought her mother was pretentious and snooty, as if she were above the plain Midwestern life of Kenosha. But Darcy knew there was more to her, deeper reasons for her acting the way she did.

Since Darcy's father had left them, when Darcy was still little, Mrs. Elliot had raised her daughter alone, on her bank-teller's salary. It was a hard life, and Darcy suspected that Paris was her mother's escape hatch—a dreamy springtime place to fantasize about through years of cold Wisconsin winters, dull conversations at the bank, and weeks when the paycheck didn't stretch quite far enough.

So although Darcy was delighted to be going to Paris, a lot of that delight was that she was going to see her mother's face when she finally saw the Eiffel Tower and the Arc de Triomphe.

"Le paté est délicieux (This paté is delicious)," Darcy said slowly—and deceitfully. She'd barely touched hers. She had that green feeling again, like she had in the cafeteria.

"Merci," her mother replied. *"C'est du foie maché aux—"*

"Haché, Mother," Darcy corrected her. "You mean it's *chopped* liver. *Foie maché* means *chewed up* liver." Just the thought sent Darcy's stomach reeling again.

"I talked to the travel agent today," her mother was saying. "She's getting us a very good fare."

Darcy tried to say something, but then decided against it. If she could just hold still and wait until the nausea passed.

"How do you find the wine?" her mother asked formally.

"Oh, I usually just look around on the table and there it is," Darcy said, managing to come up with a joke.

Her mother laughed, then said, "I'll go get the *pièce de résistance."*

Darcy waited while her mother went out to the kitchen and brought in an earthenware crock. She lifted the lid and Darcy inhaled the steam. She began to feel a little queasy.

"Oh, what is it?" Darcy asked politely.

"Coq au vin."

Darcy peered into the crock. There was another chicken swimming in another pool of liquid. There seemed to be chickens everywhere she looked lately. Her queasiness melted into a wave of nausea. She grabbed her napkin off her lap as quickly as she could, covered her mouth, and ran for the bathroom to throw up. She could hear her mother calling after her, "Darcy. There's more to life than Big Macs!"

Once inside the john, Darcy locked the door, threw up several more times and then, sitting on the tile floor, pressing her face into a cold, wet washcloth, asked herself, "What's going on? What's happening to me?"

Chapter 5

Up in her room that night, Darcy took off her jeans and rubbed the red zipper mark on her stomach. She stood sideways and looked in the mirror on her closet door to see if her stomach was any bigger.

"Hard to say," she muttered to herself. "Maybe." Then she put her hands over her breasts. "Ouch," she cried. They felt heavier, tighter—and they really were sore to the touch.

She put on her old Smurf nightgown and crawled into bed among all her "night buddies," her stuffed animals. She picked up the novel by the side of her bed—*The Sun Also Rises*—but she gave up after a few pages. She just couldn't concentrate.

She opened the drawer of her nightstand and took out her packet of birth control pills. She counted them and saw she was a couple of days behind—as usual—so she popped two. Then she pulled out her datebook and did some more counting. Then she picked up the phone and called Lila.

"Hey," she said, "will you meet me on the side steps after school tomorrow? I need you to help me with something. Yeah, kind of important."

The next afternoon, Darcy and Lila were down in a dark corner of Darcy's basement. Darcy was anxiously pacing back and forth, then stopped suddenly.

"Well?" she said, pressing Lila for some information. But Lila didn't look up. She was intent on her work—shining a flashlight on a small glass bottle.

"*Your* job," she said to Darcy, "is looking out for your mother."

In the silence, both of them listened to Mrs. Elliot upstairs in the living room, droning out responses to the woman on her *French Made E-Z* tape. Lila continued to stare at the bottle; Darcy went back to her pacing.

"It just turned pink," Lila said. "And now it's red."

Darcy rushed over to the table and snatched up the instruction folder. She read aloud from it.

"When the liquid turns dark pink to red"—here her voice suddenly brightened—"the results are *positive!*"

"Not positive *good,* you knucklehead," Lila said impatiently. "Positive *positive!*"

Darcy glared at Lila, as if staring her down would make her back down and make what she was saying not true. But Lila stuck to her guns.

"Look," she said, "I know about these things. My dad's a doctor."

"Could be a defective test," Darcy said desperately. "I told you we shouldn't have bought the generic kit."

Ignoring this, Lila poked her index finger into Darcy's breast.

"Any tenderness here?"

"Ouch!"

"Thought so," Lila said. Then, eyeing them more closely, "And they are much bigger. Almost as big as mine. Let's see, any other symptoms? Unexpected regurgitations? Frequent urination?"

"Huh?" said Darcy, who was lost in her own thoughts.

"Are you throwing up and peeing a lot?"

Darcy nodded sadly, then started to get angry.

"Damn it! I mean I was . . . I mean I go to all the trouble to *get* the pill and then . . ."

"I think you also have to *take* them," Lila said sarcastically.

"Come on. I hardly ever miss," Darcy said defensively.

"And you hardly ever get pregnant," Lila countered. "Stan know?"

Darcy just put a weary head on Lila's shoulder. And Lila just hugged her friend. There didn't seem to be any more words to cover the situation. They just stood there together in the musty basement, listening to the French tape playing upstairs.

"I am lost," the recorded voice said flatly. "Could you help me get back to the center of town?"

The next night Darcy was supposed to go to a movie with Stan. She went to meet him when he got off work at the shoe store. Mr. Bobrucz was just closing up and gave her a little flak when she came in—as usual.

"Hey, here's Darcy Elliot, Star Reporter. Doing her story on Bunions Across America." Then he shouted toward the stockroom, "Hey, Stan, your girlfriend's here." To Darcy, he said, "And tell him no funny business. I got hidden cameras back there."

Usually, Darcy would've gotten a kick out of Mr. Bobrucz's teasing, but tonight she had to force even the grimmest smile, and by the time she got back to the stockroom, even *it* was gone.

Stan was putting shoe boxes back in their slots. He looked up and saw right away, from her expression, that something was wrong.

"Hey, why the long face?"

She tried to say something, but suddenly found herself choked up, fighting down tears. Sometimes she hated her emotional side. Just when she most wanted to come across as mature and rational, she broke down and knew she seemed about ten years old.

"What *happened?"* Stan said, taking both her hands. "You wrecked your mom's car?"

"No."

"You only got a B-plus in French?"

She shook her head.

"Then it can't be *that* bad," he said, trying to console her.

"It *is*."

She watched him figure it out.

"Oh, no," he said. "You can't be. You're on the pill. When was your last period?"

"Two months ago."

"Two months!"

"I'm irregular, okay? That's why I started taking the pill in the first place. To regulate my periods."

He looked hurt and confused.

"I thought you started taking it . . . well . . . for me."

Darcy put her arms around him, expecting him to hug her back, but his arms just hung at his sides.

"I'm sorry," she said. "I didn't mean to lie to you. The doctor put me on the pill when I was fourteen. I would've started taking it for you if I wasn't already taking it. But I didn't want to tell you. I didn't want you to think I was taking it because I was trashy. You know, easy."

"Easy!" Stan moaned. "You made me wait two and a half years. How could I think you were easy?"

She sat down on a bench, shaken, feeling oddly distant from this moment. Maybe it was that she *wanted* to be far away from it.

"I never figured it would happen like this," she told him. "I knew it would be you—I knew that much.

But here . . . like this . . ." Her eyes welled up with tears.

"What're we going to do?" Stan said.

She could see from his expression that Stan didn't have any more answers than she did, that he was equally lost. For a moment, she felt like she had flown up into the sky and was looking down on the two of them from some great distance. What she saw was a guy and a girl sitting on the floor of a stockroom of a shoe store in Kenosha, Wisconsin, beginning to realize that their lives had just completely changed.

"Oh, God," she said.

Chapter 6

The next day, Darcy and Stan met Lila and Chris—their best friends—in the school cafeteria at lunchtime to talk about "The Problem." The four of them sat at a table off against the wall, away from everyone else, discussing Stan and Darcy's options. Or rather, Chris and Lila seemed to be discussing Stan and Darcy's options.

"What's the big deal about an abortion?" said Chris, stacking his burger with lettuce, tomato, and even a couple of fries.

"Lisa Jordan's had two already," Lila said, cutting a piece of her liver and onions. Lila always took Mrs. Fanelli's gruesomely nutritious hot lunch. Darcy was trying not to look at the liver, and especially not to smell it. She herself was having a can of orange soda, and she wasn't too sure she was going to be able to keep even *that* down.

"I heard that Marilyn Monroe had thirteen," Chris said, then stopped and frowned. "Who's Lisa Jordan?"

"She sits behind you in calculus," Lila said, rolling her eyes. She paused a second or two, to see if anyone else had anything to say, then plunged on. "Look, it's Darcy's decision. It's her life."

"Her life!" Chris said, indignant.

"It's *her* body," Lila countered.

"We're supposed to go to California together next year," Chris said, draping a buddy-buddy arm across

Stan's shoulders. "What's he supposed to do with *his* body. Stay home and baby-sit?"

Stan put down his sandwich, thought for a moment, then said, "Maybe Darcy can have the baby, and we can give it up for abortion."

"You mean *adoption,*" Darcy said.

"That's what I said. 'Adoption.'"

"That's what he said," Chris supported him. "'Adoption.'"

"No," Darcy said firmly, "he said 'abortion.'" She turned to Stan and looked at him steadily. "I heard you loud and clear."

"Well, you heard me wrong," Stan said defensively.

"Okay," Darcy said, in a tone of voice that both stopped the conversation and let Stan know that she didn't believe him. His slip of the tongue had made it clear what he wanted.

Three days later it was Thanksgiving. The two families were having dinner together at the Bobrucz house. All three parents were in the final stages of getting the holiday dinner on the table. The smell of turkey permeated the air. Stan and Darcy were out on the back sun porch, whispering, deep in conference.

"We can't tell them today!" Stan said. "It's Thanksgiving."

Darcy, hideously nervous, covered with a joke. "But it's perfect. Big family dinner. I can just say something along the lines of . . . 'I'm pregnant, please pass the turnips.'"

"We haven't even decided if we're going to tell them yet. Hell, we haven't even decided what we're going to do."

"Come on, kids!" Stan's mother called out as she

came into the dining room with the turkey on a platter. "Dinner!"

Darcy's mother and Stan's father followed, carrying bowls of sweet potatoes, mashed potatoes, green beans, and stuffing. Stan and Darcy reluctantly got up and joined everybody around the table.

"You know what your cousin Jimmy told me about Cal Tech yesterday?" Stan's father said to him. "Every architect has his own computer."

Everyone took his or her place around the table and sat down.

"Do you believe that?" Stan's father said. "It sure wasn't like that when I didn't go to school." He looked around and laughed heartily at his own joke.

Darcy and Stan exchanged looks. It was going to be a long afternoon.

"I hope you like my stuffing," Stan's mother said, passing the bowl around.

"The French do marvelous things to their stuffing," Darcy's mother said. "Apples, grapes, raisins."

"Mmmm, yummy," Stan's mother said.

Stan's father considered this concept for a moment, then said, "Except in the U.S.A. we don't call that stuffing, we call it fruit."

"Honey," Mrs. Bobrucz urged him, "say grace."

He grunted and took his seat at the head of the table. Everyone bowed his or her head and grew silent—well, almost everyone. All of a sudden, the pause was filled with Lou whispering hoarsely to Mary, "You don't even know what it *means*."

"Do, too. Abortion—"

"What's that?" their father said. "You know there's no talking during grace. And what's this about abortion? Where'd you hear that word? You watching those soap operas again like I told you not to?"

"She didn't hear it on a soap opera," Lou said.

"And I can't tell where I heard it . . . 'cause it's private," Mary said nervously.

"Okay," Mr. Bobrucz said. "Six Saturdays in the store stacking shoe boxes."

Mary's brown eyes welled up with tears. She looked from Stan to Darcy to her father, then back to Darcy again. This, of course, drew everyone's attention to Darcy. For a minute, she just sat there trying to think of a way out. When she couldn't, she just shrugged and blurted it out.

"I'm pregnant." She looked at her mother and Stan's parents, and Stan smiled in hopes of getting their support. Then, not able to think of anything else to follow the bomb she'd just dropped, she said, "Pass the turnips, please."

The turkey sat untouched as the moment of silence following Darcy's announcement broke into a screamfest among the parents, with Stan and Darcy lost in the shuffle.

"Abortion is not a dirty word, Mr. Bobrucz," Darcy's mother said. "It's a simple medical procedure."

"Forget abortion!" Mrs. Bobrucz said. "We give the kid up for adoption, and that's that!"

"Don't you read *Newsweek?*" Darcy's mother shouted. "Women have choices now! Darcy's future is in the balance."

"What about my son's future?" Mr. Bobrucz countered. "He has a brilliant career ahead of him. Designing schools and churches and stuff."

"Darcy and I are going to Paris next summer," Mrs. Elliot mused.

"Isn't anybody hungry?" asked Lou, holding out his plate for some turkey.

"Look, if we could all just—" Stan tried to get a word in.

"Butt out, you hear me?" his father said. "I'm tryin' to decide your future here! You know how many people would love to adopt a baby?"

"Don't be stupid," Mrs. Elliot said. "That takes care of Stan. But what about Darcy?"

"Don't call me stupid in my own house. Call your daughter stupid. She's the one who got herself in trouble."

"Oh!" Mrs. Elliot said, standing up and throwing down her napkin. "So my daughter got *herself* in trouble. Hallelujah! Another virgin birth!"

"Mom," Darcy said meekly, "would you—"

"Please," Mrs. Bobrucz said. "Let's not drag the Church into this."

"Why not? Your husband wants me to ship my little girl off somewhere so she can have this child, then give it up, and no one will be the wiser, and the family name won't be tarnished. Are you going to do this every time your son gets someone pregnant?"

"Mother . . ." Darcy said.

Then, in the middle of all this commotion, Stan asked quietly, "Why can't we just keep it?"

Everyone stared at him for a long moment, until Mr. Bobrucz finally broke the silence.

"Grow up. You had a gerbil last year. You forgot to feed it. It *died*. The kid's up for adoption . . . period."

Darcy watched helplessly as Stan sank back in defeat and once again the scene was "The Attack of the Giant Parents." Darcy felt like her mother and Stan's dad had turned into these weird monsters, lashing out at each other. As though the main problem was figuring out whose *fault* it was.

* * *

"Oh, no!" Darcy's mother was saying now. "My little girl's not going to lug a baby around for nine months and get stretch marks so you can give it up to Catholic charities."

"Oh, fine," Stan's dad said. "You're gonna commit murder so the little princess won't ruin her figure."

"What are stretch marks?" Mary asked, hoping to add to her storehouse of juicy information.

"Hi," Darcy said to Stan in a soft voice across the table.

"Hi," he said back.

"You are a selfish, unreasonable man!" Darcy's mother said to Stan's father.

"And you, Fifi, can take your French stuffing and stuff it in your ear!"

It went on like this for what seemed to Darcy like a horrible eternity and finally ended miles off the point of Stan or Darcy or the baby, with Mrs. Elliot calling Mr. Bobrucz an uncivilized peasant and Mr. Bobrucz offering Mrs. Elliot a long walk off a short pier.

Which prompted Mrs. Elliot to take a long walk out a short living room. Darcy looked across the table at Stan and shrugged.

"I'd better go home with her," she said, excusing herself. "Thanks for the din . . ." she started to say, then realized how ridiculous this was given the fact that hardly a bite of food had been eaten. "Bye," she said to Stan as her mother stormed out the door.

But Darcy didn't go anywhere. She just stood there looking at Stan. This moment was a "first" in her life. Until now, there was never any question of where her allegiance was. Although they sometimes fought and didn't always agree, Darcy loved her mother fiercely. Of course, she loved Stan, too. But until now he'd just been her high school boyfriend. Now, though, she felt linked to him in a way that was different from but as close to what she felt for her mother. And suddenly there seemed something wrong about walking out of this living room—walking out on him—now. This was their problem—hers and his, and they had to solve it *together.*

But then she heard her mother shouting from outside, "Darcy!"

And—going against her instincts—she ran out the door.

When she got to the car, her mother was sitting behind the wheel, sobbing softly.

"Not my finest hour, I'm afraid," she said, smiling an apologetic little smile at Darcy. "It's just that those Bobruczes bring out the worst in me."

"They're okay. Really." Darcy patted her mother's arm, trying to calm her down. "They're just a little different from us."

At this, Mrs. Elliot stiffened and turned and glared sharply at Darcy. "The Bobruczes are not just 'a little different from us.' They are crude, and vulgar. They are creatures from the paleolithic age of manners. They are, in a word, *déclassé*. I've always been unhappy with your associating with them. Now . . . now this. If you have that child, it's going to be part Bobrucz. A Bobruczian baby."

The mere thought of this sent her back into sobbing and Darcy back to patting her mother's arm consolingly as she thought, Maybe abortion *was* the answer. If she got one, everything would go back to the way it was before. She was tired of thinking about all of this. She'd hardly thought of anything else in weeks. It would be nice to be able to stop having to be such an *adult,* to just go back to being a teenager again.

Her mother sniffled into a hanky that she pulled

from her purse and looked over at Darcy.

"So, *ma chère,* what do you say we stop at the store, pick up a couple of frozen turkey dinners, and go home?"

"Okay."

"And tomorrow we can call Dr. Barrick and get the name of a good clinic?"

Darcy nodded the smallest nod in the world.

Chapter 7

For the next few days, Darcy felt like her fate was out of her hands. Her mother took her in to see Dr. Barrick. The night before, she had a dream that he examined her, then chuckled and said, "My dear, you're not pregnant. You just have a persistent case of indigestion." And then he gave her some giant Tums the size of Frisbees and sent her home.

In real life, though, Dr. Barrick examined her and confirmed what everyone already knew. Darcy was definitely, absolutely, undeniably, 100 percent pregnant. For the abortion, he recommended the Kenosha Medical Clinic.

"A nice place," he told Darcy and her mother. "They try to make the experience as untraumatic as possible."

Then her mother took Darcy home and made her cream of mushroom soup and a grilled cheese sandwich—her favorite lunch when she was a little girl. While they ate, Mrs. Elliot called the Kenosha Medical Clinic and made an appointment for Saturday.

When Saturday rolled around, Darcy and her mother got up and were ready way too early, so they wound up sitting for about an hour in the living room, watching out the window, listening to the ticking of the wall clock, and getting more and more nervous by the minute.

"This is the smartest thing, honey," her mother

reassured her for about the hundredth time. "It'll leave all your options open." She dabbed at a water spot on the crystal vase on the end table by her chair. "I get off work at noon. So I'll be here when . . . when you get home." She paused, then added, also for about the hundredth time, "I still think I should go with you."

Mercifully, Stan's horn honked out front, ending the wait. Darcy leapt up and grabbed her shoulder bag.

"Mother, we settled all this last night," she said as she hurried out of the house. "Stan's driving me to the clinic, and Lila's going to meet me there."

She said this in a businesslike voice, hoping to head her mother off at the emotional pass. It didn't work. Mrs. Elliot stepped in front of Darcy, blocking her way. She took her daughter's face in her hands.

"You'll be in and out of there, honey . . . you'll see." She lifted one of Darcy's hands and patted it maternally. "Thank goodness we live in the twentieth century, when modern medical science has answers to our problems."

Darcy looked hard into her mother's eyes. She pretty much understood how her mother felt. Living alone with Darcy, just the two of them, Mrs. Elliot had always confided in Darcy, treated her as much like a friend as a daughter.

Darcy knew that all the years her mother had spent in her small job in this small town, she'd been counting on Darcy to break free, become a big-time journalist, travel around the world, live the life of excitement she herself had missed out on. To her mother, the baby meant the end of all those dreams.

At first, Darcy felt bad for dashing all her mother's hopes. Then her thoughts turned over in her mind and she started to get mad. She wondered to herself, Why do I have to live my life for *her?* Why can't I just live it for *me?*

She was deep inside such thoughts all the way to the clinic. She and Stan barely exchanged a word. She got the feeling he didn't want to tamper with her decision, that his silence was a holding onto his own thoughts, to give her room to think, to make *sure* she was sure.

When they pulled up in front of the clinic, he turned off the car and asked her, "You really don't want me to go in there with you?"

Darcy shook her head. "I just want to get this over with, okay?"

They looked at each other in a more serious way than they ever had before. And then hugged each other more fiercely than they ever had before, with a complicated mix of emotions—fear, confusion, love.

"So this is the right thing—right?" Stan said, in a voice that made Darcy know he was still trying to convince himself.

"Right," she said, although she had never been *less* sure about a decision.

Suddenly there was a rap at the window. Lila.

"Hey guys, do you mind? You're not supposed to make out in front of these places."

Lila opened the door and started leading Darcy inside. Over her shoulder, she told Stan, "She'll be fine. I'll see to it personally." Seeing the look on Stan's face, she added, "Trust me. My dad's a doctor."

Inside, the waiting room was institutionally pleasant, the walls painted a calming peach and lined with rows of connected seats. In front of them were low tables with magazines and brochures fanned out on top. There were several women already there. Darcy and Lila took seats side-by-side and looked around.

"I think they're going for your basic dentist office look," Lila observed.

Darcy nodded. "They don't even call it an abortion anymore. It's a 'procedure.'" She was doing her best impersonation of bravery, but she could tell Lila wasn't buying it. She picked up a brochure and tried to find the cheery parts. "And afterwards, they give you a light snack in the recovery lounge . . ."

Darcy closed the brochure, looked at Lila, and said, "Sounds like a Club Med."

Lila, seeing through Darcy's bravado, reached over and squeezed her hand.

Darcy didn't get to the shoe store until that afternoon. As she came in, Stan was waiting on a large woman, trying to subtly persuade her out of a tiny shoe she was trying to get onto her fleshy foot.

"I think we need a size nine, Mrs. Sitwell," he was saying. Mr. Tactful.

But she rode right over his tact.

"Not on your life," she said. "I've *always* worn an eight and a half . . ." As if it were the shoe that were the problem.

Darcy flashed Stan a high sign with her eyes as she went into the stockroom to wait for him.

"Let me see if I can find . . ." Stan said, thinking fast, ". . . a larger eight and a half, Mrs. Sitwell."

He rushed into the stockroom, still holding onto Mrs. Sitwell's own shoe, and wrapped his arms lovingly around Darcy.

"Oh, honey."

She couldn't find the words to tell him what she wanted to say, so she just stood silent as he kept hugging her.

"All afternoon I was thinking about it. About him or her, I mean. A little kid with your red hair and your lips and—someday we're going to get married and have a—"

Darcy couldn't stand this anymore, so she just blurted it out: "I didn't do it."

Stan pulled back and looked at her for a long, unbelieving moment.

"I tried, okay?" she went on. "I sat in that reception room and thought about all the practical stuff. And then . . . and then I thought about this baby."

She backed away from him and started moving around the room in circles.

"I want to do it. I want to have this kid. What do you think? I know it's not for everybody, but . . ."

"But then we're not everybody," Stan said, laughing. "We're us! We're going to do it! We're going to be the best parents ever!"

"We'll get one of those backpacks. Take the kid wherever we go. What we don't know, we'll learn."

"Hey," Stan said, "how hard can it be? Billions of people do it."

"It's the right decision. I just feel so right about it," Darcy said.

"It's a great decision," he agreed. "It feels right. Everything's always been right with us—and this will be, too."

They grabbed each other and started weaving around, practically dancing between the stacks of shoe boxes.

"You really think we can do it?" Stan shouted.

"What is this—the 'Sonny and Cher show'?" It was Mr. Bobrucz. And then to Stan, he added, "Mrs. Sitwell would like her other shoe back. So she can leave."

Stan tossed his father the shoe and, when he was

out of the room, said to Darcy, "Our parents will hate it."

She nodded. "When should we tell them?"

"Now. Right away," he said.

"Wait. Hold on," Darcy said cautiously. "Maybe we should wait for a time when we're pretty sure they won't strangle us."

The problem was that neither of them wanted to go through another horrible scene. And so they just shared the baby as their special secret for a while. In an odd way, it was a nice time between them. There was something about having a secret that made them feel especially close.

Stan got a book on knitting and learned enough—well, almost enough—to knit a pair of booties. He presented them to Darcy one day after school when they were up in her room and her mother was still at work at the bank.

Darcy burst out laughing when she saw them.

"You must think this kid's going to be Bigfoot," she said, holding up the booties, which were full of holes and knots and were nearly big enough for a kid to start school in. "And if you'll pardon my asking, why are they blue? Is there some symbolism here? Some deeper meaning?"

"I'm just pretty sure it's going to be a boy," he said. "I've just got a feeling. Stan, Junior. We can call him Junior."

Darcy put her hands on her hips in mock indignation and looked at him with an expression of disbelief.

"Junior?" she said. "In the first place *I* happen to be fairly certain it's going to be a girl. And in the second place, if you think I'd ever stick any child of mine with a name like Junior—give me a break! And in the third place . . ." But by now they were laughing too hard. When she started to catch her breath, he prodded her.

"And in the third place . . . "

"And in the third place," Darcy said, holding up the booties, "what did you knit these with—hockey sticks?"

They let Lila and Chris in on the secret, but swore them to absolute silence. Neither was happy that Stan and Darcy were going ahead with the baby. They'd both been pushing for the abortion. But they were good friends and accepted the decision and didn't hassle Stan or Darcy about it.

As for their parents, Stan just told his that Darcy had gone ahead with the abortion. His mother had cried a little and his father had yelled a lot, but once that storm had passed, neither of them said any more about it, except for a short, embarrassing lecture from his father about using condoms from now on.

Darcy's mother wanted details of the abortion, but Darcy pretended that the experience was just too emotionally painful to talk about. Mrs. Elliot nodded and backed off. That she had gotten her way was the important thing to her. She just started pretending that the whole thing had never happened. They went back to their French nights and plans for their trip to Paris when Darcy graduated.

This part was hard on Darcy. All the lies involved, for one thing. Plus, she was feeling sick every morning and had to hide that. Which meant throwing up in the bathroom while she ran the shower to cover the noise, then coming downstairs and pretending to love the big, buttery, syrupy, pancake breakfast her mother had fixed. Then going back upstairs and throwing up again.

She started wearing her shirts out and kept a bulky sweater on most of the time—to hide her by-now-pretty-obviously-bulging stomach. But this scheme wasn't going to work forever. She and Stan both knew it.

"If we wait much longer," Darcy teased Stan, "the baby will arrive and we'll have to pass him off as a very small friend of ours from school. I don't think it'll work. We're going to have to find a time to tell the parental units.

"When they're in a good mood," she added.

"Right. And when they're all together."

"At Christmas dinner," she said tentatively.

"Oh, great," Stan said sarcastically. "Another fun family holiday."

Chapter 8

It was a storybook Christmas night—snow falling outside the windows of the Bobrucz living room, the tree lit up with multicolored lights, carols drifting off the stereo in the corner. Darcy and her mother had been invited back to the Bobruczes'.

"To make up for Thanksgiving," Mrs. Bobrucz had told Mrs. Elliot. "I had a talk with the old man," she said. "He's going to be on better behavior this time."

Darcy's mother was determined that she would, too.

"A lady is a lady—no matter what the circumstance," she told Darcy. "I'm just not going to let that man provoke me this time."

So far she'd kept her word. And so had Stan's father. Dinner had gone smoothly, and now they were nearly through the present-opening.

"You like it?" Stan's mother asked eagerly as Darcy's mother pulled her present out of its tissue-paper–stuffed box.

"Like it? I love it!" Mrs. Elliot exclaimed in a voice Darcy thought of as her "phony-baloney special." Then she held up the gift—a ceramic model of the Eiffel Tower.

"You can plug it in," Mrs. Bobrucz added. "It lights up and plays 'I Love Paris.'"

Darcy had to cover a smile when she saw her mother's eyes widen with dismay as she took in the total awfulness of this piece of pure kitsch.

"Thanks for the great belt, Mrs. Bobrucz," Darcy said in what she hoped was a sincere voice as she opened her own gift and pulled it out of its box. It was wide and leopard-printed in something plushy. Darcy tried to imagine a situation in her life in which she could wear this. Maybe if her life took a sudden dramatic turn and she began cocktail-waitressing in a jungle-theme bar. Other than that, no way. Mrs. Bobrucz was one of the nicest women in the world, but with the least sense of style. Now she was saying, "I saw it in the store and said to myself, 'Who has a waist that little? Our Darcy!'"

Not anymore, thought Darcy, who had become a genius at disguising her expanding waist. Thank goodness for the 'big shirt' look. She had one on now, covering the spandex stomach of what no one else knew were maternity jeans.

Darcy looked up and saw Stan looking at her from across the room with question marks in his eyes. Was this the moment to tell them? Darcy nodded, took a deep breath, and prepared to plunge in, but then Mr. Bobrucz came into the room carrying a tray with glasses and a bottle of wine and took over the conversation.

"Well, she gets her figure from her mother," he said, setting down the wine and giving Darcy's mother a big hug and a wet kiss on the cheek. "Merry Christmas, Donna!" he said. "And now—a toast!"

He poured the wine into glasses, even giving one to Stan and to Darcy—causing Lou and Mary to chime in simultaneously with, "Can we have some, too?"

In the holiday spirit, he poured them each a glass with about two drops in it, and then, in the gruff voice he used to couch his affection, shooed them off, saying, "Go put some ginger ale in it!"

Then he turned back to the rest of them, held his glass aloft, and said, "You know, it's great that Stan and Darcy got us all together like this. Today, we let bygones be bygones. Because in the end—there's nothing like family!"

They all clinked their glasses as Mr. Bobrucz proclaimed the toast: "To family!"

Stan seized the moment. "Speaking of family, Dad. We're going to have one."

Everyone stopped in mid-toast and looked at him with confusion.

"A family. Me and Darcy."

"Good. Great. God bless you," Mr. Bobrucz said.

"I mean now," Stan said.

"What are you talking about?" his father demanded.

"We're going to keep it," Darcy said softly. "Stan and I are going to have the baby." She looked over at her mother, who was staring at her with a dazed look.

"You lied to me," Mrs. Elliot said in stunned disbelief.

"I didn't lie," Darcy said. "When I came home from the clinic you asked me how it went, and I said it wasn't bad."

"But you didn't do anything," her mother said.

"That's why it wasn't bad," Darcy said weakly.

Stan jumped in with his heartiest manner. "We haven't worked out *all* the details, but—"

His father's face grew nearly as red as the wine he was holding. *"Details!* How's *this* for a detail? Your future's going down the sewer!"

"Come on, Dad," Stan said. "We were *going* to do it, anyway. It's just that we're starting our future . . . now."

"Well," Mrs. Bobrucz mused, "*we* got married young."

"We were kids," Mr. Bobrucz said.

"Maybe we could raise the baby till the kids get out of school," Mrs. Bobrucz suggested.

"You're talkin' stupid!" her husband shouted. "You open your mouth, and garbage comes out."

Darcy gasped. "What an ugly, horrible thing to say!"

Mr. Bobrucz turned to her. "Hey," he jeered, "you gotta learn to keep your *mouth* shut—and your *legs* crossed."

At this, Stan leapt off the sofa and stood in front of his father.

"No! No more!"

He shoved his father into the Christmas tree, which started to topple. Mrs. Bobrucz and Mrs. Elliot grabbed it in the nick of time as Stan's father glowered at his son.

"Get out! Get out of my house!"

Stan grabbed his jacket off the coat tree in the hall, came back, and shouted at his dad, "Hey, I left. You didn't throw me out. I left."

As he moved toward the door, his father followed, shaking with anger. "And don't ever come around here asking for a handout!"

Stan's reply to this was the loud slamming of the front door.

Mrs. Elliot's approach was the opposite—calm, reasonable, and completely maddening to Darcy.

"Darcy, dear," she was saying in her coolest tone, "this is not a creative approach."

"Mother!"

"It is a mundane, pedestrian decision."

"Mother!"

"And what about Paris?"

Clapping her hands over her ears—a trick she

probably hadn't used since she was ten—Darcy screamed, "Mother . . . SHUT UP!"

She took down her hands and opened her eyes and saw that she had shocked her mother, who was now looking at her as if she were a stranger. Darcy looked back at her. Two people caught in a complicated silence. There was way too much to say, and at the same time, nothing at all to be said. In the end, Darcy just calmly got up and followed Stan out the door.

She caught up with him as he was getting into the Volvo. He turned and looked a little surprised to see her.

"Where you going?" he asked.

"With you."

"Go back before you get in more trouble."

"Can't," she said. "I just told my mother to shut up. First time in my life."

Stan looked at Darcy and broke into a slow grin.

"You did? Well, then, come on. Get in the car."

As they drove off, Darcy said, "It felt kind of good."

That night, they stayed in the Land o' Nod Motel out by the highway. The two of them sat on the worn chenille spread of the sagging double bed and pooled all their worldly goods—savings accounts, birthday money from relatives, the contents of Darcy's piggy bank.

"Well," Stan said, "with the cash . . . both savings accounts and most important of all . . . these McDonald's gift certificates . . ."

"And my Sweet Sixteen money," Darcy said, adding the check from inside a glittery card to the stash.

"Okay," Stan said, totaling it all up. "All told, we've got nine hundred twenty-seven dollars . . . and . . . six Big Macs."

"Nine hundred dollars!" Darcy got excited. "We're practically rich!" She grabbed him and rolled him over on the bed, onto the floor. When she was down on the floor on top of him, she gazed into his eyes and said dreamily, "What more on this whole entire planet could we possibly need?"

Stan barely hesitated a second before he added, realistically, "More money."

"Our first whole night together," he said later, when they'd turned off the lights and he was shivering up next to Darcy under the thin spread. "Aside from The Fateful Night—you know, before The Fateful Morning."

"Boy," Darcy said, remembering, "that seems like a million years ago and a dozen galaxies away. The storm, the tent. I hope you still have that tent. It looks like we may be needing it. To live in. I don't think either of us can go home now."

She turned over and she and Stan lay there snuggled like two spoons for a while, both of them thinking separate thoughts that spun into the dark winter night and out into their future.

Chapter 9

After three days of looking for an apartment, finding everything they liked *way* out of their price range, Stan and Darcy stood on the sidewalk in front of the Scrub-A-Dub-Dub Laundromat looking up at an APT FOR RENT sign in a steamed-up window on the second floor. Slowly, they went in the door and trudged up the sagging wooden steps. Mrs. Kramer, the landlady, was waiting for them on the landing.

"You the young couple come to look at the place?" she said brusquely. She was a heavyset woman in an old floral dress and a ratty cardigan pulling tight at the buttons. She looked like it was a big imposition on her, having to show this apartment.

Stan and Darcy nodded.

"I hope you wasn't expecting Buckingham Palace," she said, brushing past them to unlock the door. She pushed it open and Darcy and Stan went inside.

It was awful. The walls were greasy with soot, the linoleum floor was worn away in vast patches and was an ugly orange-and-green-flecked pattern, where there *was* any pattern. The windows were either steamed over from the laundromat below or covered with yellowed pull-down shades. In the kitchen, there were still dirty dishes stacked in the sink from the previous tenant. But by far the most alarming aspect of the place—at least as far as Darcy was concerned—was the toilet. It wasn't in a bathroom, just sitting all by itself in the middle of the living room.

Stan, sounding very grown-up, asked Mrs. Kramer how much the rent was.

"Hundred seventy-five a month," she told them. Stan and Darcy exchanged looks and nodded at each other. It was the first place they'd seen that they could realistically afford. He handed Mrs. Kramer three hundred fifty in cash—the first month's rent plus a security deposit, although it seemed impossible anyone could leave this place in worse shape than it was now. Doing *anything* to it would have to be an improvement.

Mrs. Kramer didn't seem surprised that they took the apartment, nor did she seem particularly excited to have them as tenants. She just started reciting the rules of the building:

"No pets. No loud music. Any parties after ten at night—you're out! Rent's due the first of the month. If I don't get it—you're out! No tap dancing, no loud arguments, no bowling. And no drugs. I catch you with drugs—you're out!"

"Uh, excuse me," Darcy interjected politely. "But has that toilet been moved out of the bathroom for repairs or something? I mean, I don't see the bathroom, but I assume there is one."

Mrs. Kramer, who was counting out Stan's money, looked up distractedly and said, "Huh? Oh, no. That there's your powder room," she said, nodding toward the lone toilet. "And of course you've got your tub in kit."

"Our what?" Darcy asked.

"Under the counter in the kitchen, there's your bathtub. Enjoy," she said as she lumbered off down the stairs.

Stan waited a half-second, then leaned over and kissed Darcy. She backed off in mock propriety.

"Better watch it. She didn't mention kissing, but it might be that if she catches us at it . . ."

Stan picked up the joke and finished Darcy's sentence:. . . "We're out!"

They walked around the apartment a little, trying to find some good features to it. Darcy fell into total despair. She couldn't stand even being here, couldn't imagine *living* here. All she could think of was her bedroom at home—all peach and white with her canopy bed by the window that overlooked Mrs. Green's peonies next door.

"Our happy home," Stan said brightly from the kitchen. "On the plus side, the laundry facilities couldn't be closer. On the negative side—well, everything else. But a little cleaning up and it should be quite cozy."

"Clean it?" Darcy said. "Are you kidding? I'd say the kitchen alone would take a gallon of Fantastik, a dozen cans of E-Z Off, and a small nuclear device—just for starters."

"Come on," Stan cajoled her. "Let's give it a try. Let's go get some supplies, and then sneak over for our clothes and stuff. Once we've got our things in here, it'll seem a lot more possible. Trust me."

"Okay," Darcy said dubiously, then fell silent. "What's that noise?" she said after a minute. Stan stood still until he, too, heard it. Thump, thump. Thump, thump.

"Somebody's got their tennis shoes in the dryer," he said.

They spent the afternoon out with Chris in his pickup truck. After they picked up cleaning supplies, they stopped by Darcy's for her things. This went fine. Her mother was still at the bank, and none of the Carters, who lived in the other side of the duplex, was around to get nosy. They were in and out in half an hour with no one the wiser.

"Do you want to leave her a note or something?" Stan asked.

Darcy shook her head.

"I'm still too mad at her for trying to run my life like it was hers. Anything I'd write would just be poison."

Stan and Chris dropped Darcy off at the apartment and went over to the Bobrucz house to get Stan's stuff. First they got his clothes, stereo, and drafting table on the truck, then they hauled out the mattress from Stan's bed.

"That's great," Stan was saying to Chris as they leaned the mattress onto the truck bed. "You'll be my best man. And one more thing . . ."

"What?"

"I want you to be the kid's godfather."

"Godfather?" Chris said dubiously. "That doesn't mean I have to change any dirty diapers, does it?"

"Don't worry," Stan said, putting a hand on Chris's shoulder, "it's under control. Soon as the little sucker shows up, we're going to housebreak it."

As they were talking, there was a whoosh of tires as Mr. Bobrucz pulled into the driveway. Seeing Stan, he slammed on the brakes and jumped out of the car.

"Great timing," Stan said to Chris.

"Oh, no," his father said, coming over, waving dramatically. "Nope. Off the truck with that."

"It's *my* mattress," Stan said firmly.

"Oh, it is, huh? Well, I suppose it *is* yours in the sense that you used to wet it. But you didn't pay for it."

"I never wet this bed," Stan protested. "I wet the

bed that Lou got." As he said this, Stan let go of the mattress. It sagged against Mr. Bobrucz, throwing him off-balance.

"I'll buy my own damn bed," Stan shouted. "With my own money!"

He and Chris hopped into the cab of the truck. As they drove off, Stan shouted out the window. "You're a sweetheart, Dad! Really love you a lot . . ."

"I know. I'm a real jerk, right? My son shoves me into a Christmas tree and *I'm* the jerk!" Then he stood looking at the unwieldy, wobbling mattress, clearly wondering how he was going to get it back into the house, and muttered to himself, "They used to put handles on these things!"

Back at the apartment, Darcy was losing her good nature, fast.

"There's only one closet in this whole place," she told Stan despairingly as she shoved her clothes onto the pole next to his. "Actually, I don't know why I brought all this stuff over, anyway. I can't fit into any of it. What am I going to do? I can't afford a whole new wardrobe of maternity clothes."

She could feel herself starting to cry and hated herself for it. It seemed like every time that she ran into a hard situation lately, instead of acting calm, cool, and tough-minded, she took on the consistency of Silly Putty.

Stan came over and put an arm around her. "Hey, don't worry about the cosmic issues right now. I've got a very specific and immediate question you've got to answer."

"What?" Darcy said, sniffling.

"Do you know what tonight is?"

"Thursday?"

"Good try. It's Wednesday. It's also New Year's Eve."

"Oh, boy," she said. "I didn't even think of it. Last year it would've been one of the most important dates on my calendar."

"Well," Stan went on, "speaking of dates, I don't have one. So, well I know it's last minute, but . . . would you be mine? My New Year's Eve date?"

"That depends," Darcy said, pretending to be coy. "Just what'd you have in mind? Renting a private jet and taking me to Paris for champagne on top of the Eiffel Tower?"

"Close," Stan said. "Definitely a party for two. But in your condition, I think sparkling apple juice instead of champagne. And instead of the Eiffel Tower, an equally intimate setting, and one much closer . . ."

". . . to the laundry facilities!" Darcy filled in, and they both started laughing.

The streets were filled with New Year's Eve revelers when Stan went out to shop for their celebration. By the time he trudged up the stairs to the apartment with the apple juice, some take-out chicken, and a carton of chocolate chocolate-chip ice cream, well-wishers had plunked a party hat on his head and thrust a paper whistle into his hand.

He thought he looked pretty irresistible, entering the apartment wearing the hat and blowing on the whistle, but Darcy wasn't there to appreciate the sight. She was, he could tell from the sound of water running, taking a makeshift shower. Well, if that was where she wanted to celebrate New Year's Eve, it was fine with him. He quickly stripped and climbed into the tub.

Stan expected Darcy to be surprised at his invasion

of her shower, but he didn't expect her to seem . . . well . . . embarrassed.

"What's wrong?" he asked as she turned to face the wall. "What's the matter?"

"Nothing," she answered, shaking her head. "It's just . . . I've never seen you . . . nude."

"Get out!"

"No. I mean, we *did* it . . . but we could never wait till we got our clothes off."

Slowly, almost shyly, Darcy turned to face him. As they looked at each other as if for the first time, Stan whispered softly into Darcy's ear, "Want to get married on Valentine's Day?"

Darcy pulled back from Stan and said coldly, "We don't *have* to."

"I know. I *want to*. Don't you?"

"Yeah," she said, trying to hide her hurt.

"What's the matter?" he said, bending down, trying to look deeper into her eyes.

"Nothing," she lied.

Stan thought for a minute, then smiled and said, "I think I see what the problem is, the missing ingredient." And with that, he dropped to one knee, took Darcy's hand, and said, "Darcy Elliot . . . will you do me the honor of being my wife?"

Darcy tried to say yes, but there was a knot in her throat. All she could do was nod through the mix of water and tears streaming down her cheeks.

Chapter 10

The week after New Year's, Stan went over to Kolby's Shoes. Ed Kolby was Mr. Bobrucz's biggest competitor.

"You got any shoe store experience?" Mr. Kolby asked Stan when he told him he wanted part-time work.

"Six years."

"Hmmm. Well, I'm always looking for good people with experience. But wait a minute, aren't you Vic Bobrucz's kid?"

"Yes, sir."

"Then why do you want to work for *me?*"

"My father fired me."

"Okay, you start Friday after school," Mr. Kolby said. "Boy, your dad is *really* going to be teed off."

"Yeah," Stan said, smiling, "I know."

Mr. Kolby patted Stan on the back and began to smile, too.

Every day after school, while Stan was working at Kolby's, Darcy was at the school paper. Today though, while the other kids at light boxes were laying out the *Clarion,* Darcy and Lila were working on another sort of document.

Their friend Marnie Davis came in with a stack of envelopes. "Here they are," she said. "The invitations came back from the instant-print place. How's the marriage license coming?"

Darcy peeled the doctored license off the light box and showed her.

"Not bad, eh?" she said proudly. "Anybody need a passport or driver's license?"

Lila opened the invitations.

"Oh, they look great!" She showed one to Darcy, whose heart stopped for a second. There it was, all neatly printed on a cream-colored card. It was really happening. She was getting married.

"Darcy Elliot and Stanley Bobrucz request the pleasure of your company at their marriage . . ." she read aloud. "Wow."

Lila grabbed the stack out of Darcy's hands and started passing them out.

"Wedding invitations! It's next Saturday. I'm maid of honor, and there's a party after."

All the girls in the room gathered around.

"Oh, this is so cool!"

"I'll definitely be there."

"Can we bring dates?"

"You're the first person I ever knew who got married."

Darcy looked around. Suddenly all these girls, whom she'd grown up with, gone through grade school, junior high, and high school with, whose problems and secrets and gossip she'd shared for years—suddenly seemed far away from her, and much much younger. Then she realized it wasn't they who'd moved away—it was she.

"Uh, do you guys know I'm . . . uh . . . pregnant?" She was hoping they'd all look flabbergasted, but they just nodded.

"Uh-huh."

"Yeah."

"Right."

"Mmmhmm."

"Bet the whole damn school knows," Darcy said, just kidding. But they took the wind out of Darcy's sails by saying all together, "Yeah."

This was not thrilling news. Although she had gossiped about everyone else in this school, Darcy had never really thought of people gossiping about *her*. Yet, clearly, talk had been going on behind her back. She wondered what they'd been saying? Probably better she didn't know.

Everyone was full of questions.

"Have you picked out any names yet?"

"Oh, if it's a girl, you've just got to call her Jessica."

"Are you still going to college?"

"No, not Jessica—Krystle."

At this point, Darcy felt compelled to speak up. "That is *so* queer. I am *not* naming it Krystle."

Suddenly she crossed her legs and wrapped her arms around her stomach. "Ooooo, I can't believe I've got to go *again!*" she said and rushed out to the girls' lavatory. She went into the back stall. While she was in there, Michaela and her best friend Elaine came in talking to each other.

"Michaela, you lie," Darcy heard Elaine say.

"I do not."

"You went out with Stan Bobrucz?"

"Eighth grade. We were children . . . but now he's so mature . . ." Michaela purred. "So deep."

Then Darcy heard the "ssssss" of a match lighting, and the smell of a cigarette being lit.

"So what do you think?" Elaine asked, exhaling loudly. "They going to kick the 'Mother of the Year' out of school?"

"You kidding?" Michaela said. "Miss Congeniality? Please."

"I don't suppose we'll get to read about *this* in her precious little newspaper."

"I just love it when the smart kids turn out to be so stupid," Michaela said, which made Elaine choke on her cigarette and both of them crack up.

Darcy sat in the back stall—absolutely still and utterly humiliated.

In January, the winter, which had been mild so far, went into a cold snap. Darcy sat at her electric typewriter with mittens on her hands and a bulky wool scarf around her neck. She was practically on top of the room's one small radiator, which barely put out enough heat to warm a muffin. She wasn't thinking about her immediate surroundings at the moment, though. She was deep into her fantasies of journalistic glory.

"I'm going to write about the kid," she told Stan, who was across the room, prying an old grate off the wall. "Everything I feel as I go along. I'll show that Markus in Madison. I'll get gritty. I'll get real." She stopped talking to receive a flash from her brain. "I know. I'm going to call it 'Inside Out.'"

She pulled out of her reverie to see Stan—also in his jacket and gloves—rigging up a winch with a car jack and ropes.

"Honey," she said, "you really think that's going to work?"

"The dryers downstairs in the laundromat get all this excess heat. It has to go somewhere. My hunch is that it goes into the pipes."

"I read Robert Frost to the baby this morning," Darcy told him when he'd set back to work. "The kid couldn't get into it, though. Tomorrow I'm going to try Dr. Seuss."

"Always good to start with the classics," he said.

"There won't be any fumes, will there?" Darcy asked, getting up from the desk and coming across the room to inspect this experiment.

"No, I checked. They're *electric* dryers."

"I'm marrying a genius."

"Darcy, I need some extra muscle here."

She helped him by taking hold of one of the ropes and, as he counted down, "Three . . . two . . . one!" they both gave a big yank and the vent gave way, followed by a blizzard of tiny, snowlike particles. Stan threw his gloves into the air.

"Heat!" he said.

"Lint!" Darcy said as they raised their arms and began dancing in a circle, like Indians finally getting their rain.

Chapter 11

Whenever Darcy had imagined getting married, Stan was always the groom in the fantasy. But an *older* Stan—slightly more mature and worldly-wise, starting up his own architectural firm. She was older in the fantasy, too—self-possessed and sophisticated, a reporter for a major newspaper, on call for fast-breaking stories all over the world. They'd come back to Kenosha for the wedding so their families could be there, so Darcy could walk down the aisle of the beautiful Episcopalian church on a sunny June day in her grandmother's heirloom lace-and-satin gown.

Her *actual* wedding day turned out quite a bit differently. For one thing, she was seventeen, not a hot-shot reporter for anything except her high school paper. No parents or family were present for the ceremony, and the church was filled with their friends from school, the only people who had accepted Stan and Darcy's decision.

The bride was not wearing her grandmother's gown. She was several months beyond being able to fit into a wedding gown. And they hadn't even dared approach the Episcopalian church with their fake marriage license. The only recognized minister they could find in all of Kenosha who was willing to perform the ceremony with no questions asked was Reverend Kim, fresh from Korea, pastor of Reverend Kim's Church of Southeast Asian Christian Fellowship.

And finally, it was *not* a beautiful sunny June day

—it was a blizzard in the middle of February.

The only thing about this wedding that was the same as her fantasy was Stan, waiting for her with Chris and Lila at the front of the church as she walked down the aisle. Midway, she realized that she was tracking up the white runner with her snowy boots and stopped to slip them off—making the rest of the trip in her socks, tears streaming down her cheeks.

She supposed that everyone watching would take these for the standard bridal tears of joy. But they were really a mixture of several kinds of tears. Joy was in there, of course. What girl could be marrying the guy she loved and not have some tears of joy? But there were also tears of frustration at the way her life had been cut up like a jigsaw puzzle with no way of knowing what the picture would look like once those pieces were all put together again.

There were also tears of regret that her mother wasn't here, or Stan's parents. And a few other tears were, Darcy knew, a bittersweet farewell to someone she liked—the girl Darcy. Now she was stepping into the outline of a new Darcy—a wife and mother—a person she didn't know and wasn't sure she was really ready to be.

When she was standing next to her bridegroom, Reverend Kim smiled down on them and nodded toward Stan.

"Pleasa to geve Darcy de ling," he said.

Chris extended his forefinger to Stan; the ring was on its tip, and Stan pulled it off.

"Pleasa to say affa me: I gee yoo dees ling assa sigh ob owa fay, hoh an lob."

Stan looked at Reverend Kim in bewilderment.

Darcy whispered to Stan an interpretation: "I give

you this ring as a sign of our faith, hope, and love."

"Oh," Stan whispered back. "Boy, this guy's English is terrible."

"He's been here only three months," Darcy said. "Imagine how bad your Korean would be."

Stan nodded and said out loud, looking sincerely at Darcy, "I give you this ring as a sign of our faith, hope, and love." Then he stood there smugly, feeling pretty good about his performance.

"Give me the ring," Darcy whispered.

"Oh," Stan said, realizing he was leaving something out. "Here." He fumbled in his nervousness but finally got it on Darcy's ring finger, at which point Reverend Kim said, "May ee boong owa harks ang rybes."

Stan and Darcy looked at each other and shrugged. Neither of them could make out this one.

"Excuse me, sir?" Stan said, and Reverend Kim repeated, "May ee boong owa harks ang rybes."

Darcy suddenly got it and whispered hurriedly to Stan, "May it bind our hearts and lives."

"Oh," Stan said, moved by the sentiment, "that's so nice."

"Say it," Darcy prompted him.

"May it bind our hearts and lives."

As he said this, Darcy looked down at her ring for the first time. Then she looked back up at Stan, with tears in her eyes.

"What's the matter?" he said, then looked down with her.

The ring, which he'd gotten at the dime store, was so thin it had already bent. He squeezed it, more or less bending it back into shape.

"I'm sorry," he told Darcy. "I'll get you another one—a real ring—as soon as we can afford it."

"Yes?" Darcy said.

"I promise," Stan said, then looked up at Reverend Kim and asked, "Are we married yet?"

"Married," Reverend Kim said. "Yes, married."

"Then I guess I'd better kiss the bride," he said to Darcy. "And you'd better kiss the groom."

Which they did—to the wild cheering of all their friends. Suddenly, the solemn occasion broke into a totally rowdy burst of congratulations. Lila gave Darcy a big hug, and Chris gave Stan one. All the other kids piled out of the pews, into the aisles. Retro stood up on one of the seats holding his boom box and announced, "Ladies and gentlemen! The official wedding song . . ."

He punched the play button and suddenly the church was filled with "She's Having My Baby."

"Boo!"

"Hiss!" They all responded, throwing their hats and scarves at him as they started down the aisle and out of the church.

When they got to the front door, Stan picked Darcy up into his arms and carried her down the snowy steps. Falling all around them was snow, mixed with the rice that was being tossed by all their friends. Darcy threw her head back and laughed.

"Hey, this getting married is kind of fun," she said to Stan, kissing him on the cheek.

"Yeah, we ought to do it more often," he said, and then to everyone gathered around on the steps of the church, "You are all formally invited to a reception at the abode of marital bliss—our new apartment."

"Where is it?" someone shouted.

"Just find the Scrub-A-Dub-Dub Laundromat . . . and then follow the lint."

Although it didn't make the society pages of the Kenosha paper, Darcy knew her wedding reception would definitely go down in the history of everyone there as one of the great parties of their lives.

The music was provided by Retro's boom box, the dancing by everyone. The cake came from a mix and was decorated by Lila with a heart, a model of G.I. Joe, and a pregnant Barbie Doll.

Everyone brought gifts—whatever they could. Darcy surveyed the loot—a toaster, an iron, some pots, and a set of dishes. A wok. She opened the box on her lap and looked inside.

"A head of lettuce?" she said. "Just what I've always wanted. Thanks a million, Retro."

"It's plastic," he said. "You keep it in your refrigerator. To hide your money and jewels." He came over to show her, unscrewing the bottom and pointing inside.

"See," he said. "Until you get money and jewels, I filled it with licorice."

Darcy pulled out a string of licorice and passed the lettuce head to Marnie, then gave Retro a hug. Under his weirdness, he was sometimes surprisingly sweet.

Then she looked over to see Stan pulling something out of a huge Hefty bag tied with a satin bow. It was a baby bassinet.

"It's from Chris and Marnie," he said, reading the tag.

"It was my brother's," Chris said. "He's moved up to a Harley."

Darcy went over and pulled a book out of the basinette.

"Thank You, Dr. Lamaze," she read the title.

"For when you're in labor," Marnie said. "It was my sister's."

Darcy hugged Marnie and Chris as Lila came up and gently set her gift on Darcy's lap. "It's an old 1940s-style manual typewriter."

"My gift's not for the baby," she said shyly. "It's for you. For your article. I wanted you to have something from the great old tradition of newspapers."

"Oh, Lila," Darcy said in a voice made small by all the emotions tumbling through her at the moment. "This is too much."

"Hey, I just found it in my attic," Lila said, suddenly getting bashful herself.

Darcy looked down and saw that there was already a sheet of paper rolled onto the typewriter's platen. She read it out loud:

" 'Inside out,' by Darcy Elliot." She smiled, then went on. "Dedicated to my devoted friend, Lila, without whom this article would have been written on a crummy electric with no character or tradition at all."

She looked over at her best friend and felt tears welling up in her eyes.

Later, when Darcy was dancing with a bunch of the old gang, she looked over and saw Stan and Chris eating a piece of wedding cake off the same plate. From where she was, she couldn't hear what they were saying, but it looked serious.

"So what're you going to do when your scholarship comes through?" was what Chris was actually saying.

"*If* it comes through," Stan said.

"You and Darcy talk about it?"

"I think she's afraid to bring it up," Stan said.

"Oh, yeah," Chris said sarcastically. "*Darcy's* afraid to bring it up."

"Hey, you guys, break up this seriousness." It was Marnie, holding a champagne bottle. "You've got important frivolous party duties to attend to. Like for instance, opening this."

Everyone gathered around as Chris popped the cork and filled Styrofoam cups with frothing champagne. Camping it up, like a master of ceremonies, he said, "As the best man, whaddaya say to a coupla craz*eee* kids?"

Marnie, sensing a toast coming up, went over and turned down the volume on Retro's boom box. Chris got serious as he fumbled around for the right thing to say.

"You want to say how you feel without being a Hallmark card, right?" He raised his cup. "So I guess I'll keep it short and sweet. To Stan and Darcy. . ."

Then, just as he was about to give his heartfelt toast, right into the middle of this moving moment, came the bellowing voice of Mrs. Kramer, the landlady:

"It's ten o'clock. The party's over. . .or you're out!"

By midnight, Stan had finished tying up the last garbage bag, washed the last glass, and made his way across the apartment to Darcy, who was stretched out on the bed resting. She was wearing one Walkman on her head and had an extra pair of headphones on her stomach—for the baby. The tape she had on was Debussy's *Water Suite*.

Stan flopped onto the bed next to her and pulled the earphones off her head. "Hey, Slim. How's the alien?"

She looked up at him.

"Scared?" he asked.

She looked away and said, "A little."

But he knew her too well, five years' worth. He wasn't about to let her off the hook that easily.

"Are you lying?" he asked.

"A little," she admitted. She turned over onto her

back and bunched some pillows up behind her and tried to explain to him the feelings that were bouncing around inside her. "I had this doll once. Wendy Wets." She smiled at the memory. "It peed."

Stan laughed in amazement.

"No, I'm serious," she said. "It came with diapers and everything. And then . . . then there was Tiny Tears. She cried real tears. And Chatty Cathy. She talked when you pulled a string on her back."

Stan snuggled in with her, listening, putting his arms around her swollen stomach as she said, "I just never had a doll that did everything at once, see."

They looked at each other for a long moment, both feeling the heavy weight of parenthood settle over them. Then Stan said suddenly, "I felt it! It moved. Inside you!"

Darcy lifted her head to look at her stomach, then sank back against the pillows again, her hand on Stan's.

"Yeah," she said, "it's not a concept anymore. Or an issue. Or a problem. Pretty soon it's going to be a person."

Chapter 12

Darcy was in the middle of the living room floor, assembling the crib she and Stan had bought at a warehouse store, when the phone rang.

"Hello?" she said, picking up the receiver on the wall phone in the kitchen, kind of hoping it was her mother calling to apologize. She kind of hoped this every time the phone rang.

"Mrs. Darcy Lynn Elliot-Bobrucz?" It was Stan.

"This is she," Darcy said, then giggled. "I mean, this is *them*." She started drawing little baby feet in the frost on the window. The past couple of weeks, Darcy had slid into a mellow phase about the baby. Maybe this wasn't going to change her life all that much—except for the better. She loved living with Stan. So far, their savings and wedding present money was holding out. She'd gotten past her queasiness. She was keeping up with her schoolwork and putting in her regular amount of time on the newspaper. So what was the big deal, really?

"It's your husband," Stan said, "who has made exactly three sales all day. I can't get the hang of Kolby's sales pitch . . ."

Then Darcy heard Mr. Kolby calling Stan: "Hey Bobrucz! You got a blonde out here!"

Stan cupped his hand over the phone so Darcy couldn't hear the rest, then asked Mr. Kolby, "A what?"

"A customer," Mr. Kolby said, then added sarcastically, "Maybe."

"Got to go," Stan told Darcy. "The wide world of footwear calls."

"Yeah," she said. "I heard. See you for dinner. I'm cooking."

"Oh, no!" Stan teased.

"Yeah, I'm trying to figure out what people did before the microwave. There's this funny big metal box here in the kitchen. With these little fires on top. I think I'm on the verge of a big discovery."

Stan laughed and then hung up and went to see just what Mr. Kolby meant by "customer."

It was Michaela, looking—or so she said—for a new pair of Reeboks.

"Ummm. This one doesn't feel quite right," she said about the first pair Stan brought out. "But I like the way it felt when you put it on my foot."

Stan looked over to see Mr. Kolby raising an eyebrow at this conversation. Michaela, however, was oblivious—totally on her own track.

"So—how's married life?" she asked Stan in a voice dripping with curiosity.

"Good. Good," Stan said nervously. "It's good." He looked over to see Mr. Kolby waving his hand in a gesture that said "Hurry up—make a sale."

"Uh, how about this style?" Stan said, pulling a shoe from another box, slipping it onto Michaela's foot as fast and businesslike as he could.

"You busy later?" she asked sweetly. "My parents are sort of out of town."

"I'm going home to dinner," Stan said.

"Ouch!" Michaela squealed, to show how tight this shoe was. Stan pulled it off.

"Maybe after? I figure Darcy's probably going to a Tupperware party or something."

"Look, Michaela, it doesn't look like there's anything here for you, okay?" Stan said, pointing at the boxes on the floor around them, but trying to make it clear that he was talking about more than just shoes. Then he looked down and saw that he was absent-mindedly still holding onto her bare foot. He dropped it like a hot potato. All he could think of now was getting her out of this store—customer or not. So he added, unfortunately loud enough for Mr. Kolby to hear, "Besides, Michaela, we close in five minutes. There's really not enough time to show you anything else."

Michaela slipped on her own shoes and stood up smoothly, unruffled by this rejection.

"Maybe next time, Stan," she said smiling. "Maybe we'll find a fit."

When she was out the door, Stan turned to Mr. Kolby, shrugged helplessly, and said, "I'm sorry, sir. She's sort of a problem."

"*Now* she's a problem, kid," Mr. Kolby said, furious. "A minute ago she was a customer."

Darcy was coming out of her fifth-period English class the next day, talking with Lila about the papers they'd just gotten back.

"An A," Lila said, pulling Darcy's paper away from her. "You must get bored getting them all the time. Don't you ever long for a B—just to break the monotony?"

"Emily Dickinson's my favorite poet," Darcy said. "Writing about her is a breeze. But next week—Thomas Wolfe. The book is so *long!*"

"The title seems extremely relevant to your life at the moment, though," Lila pointed out.

"*You Can't Go Home Again,*" Darcy said, reading from the book cover. "Yeah. Right."

"Darcy! Darcy!" Someone was running up behind them in the hall. It was Samantha Gregory, one of the hall monitors.

"Yeah?" Darcy said, turning.

"Ms. Giles wants to see you in her office. Now."

Darcy flashed a question-mark look at Lila. What could the guidance counselor want to see her about?

"Maybe she's going to tell me to put off my dream of becoming a ballerina for the next few months," Darcy joked.

"They probably just lost your entire transcript in the school computer—like they did to Dave Simmons," Lila teased. "See you after school?"

"Right," Darcy said. "Meet you on the west steps."

The few other times Darcy had been to see Ms. Giles—to get advice on various colleges—she'd been fun and friendly, a casual-type person. Today, though, as Darcy came into her office, Ms. Giles looked up from her computer with an expression that was a mix of tension and sadness, the kind of look the doctor comes out of the operating room with when he has to tell the family that Grandma died.

"Hi, Darcy," she said, waving toward the chair in front of the desk. "Have a seat."

Darcy sat down slowly—sitting and getting up were getting to be tricky propositions lately—and waited nervously. She had no idea what Giles wanted.

"Look, Darcy," she said. "You and I have always been straight with each other. What I have to tell you is that I think—at this point—night school would be the best idea for you. For everyone."

Darcy couldn't believe her ears. What was going on here? Was she being thrown out of school?

"Maybe you don't understand, Ms. Giles," she

said, trying to make her voice calmer than she felt. "I'm going to have this baby, and then I'm going to college—just like we talked about before. And then I'm going to be a reporter and—"

"Good! Do it all! Go for it! Night school isn't going to stop you."

Suddenly the little alarm on Ms. Giles' wristwatch went off. She looked down at it as if it were a pesky fly that had just landed on her wrist.

"Darn, I'm late. We'll have to pick this up in the morning. Be here at eight," she said as she picked up her shoulder bag and practically flew out of her office. This was Giles's basic style—young woman in a hurry. Darcy decided two could play that game and ran after her, out into the faculty parking lot.

"Ms. Giles? Ms. Giles," she shouted as she caught up with her, "you don't have any right to advise me to quit school. It's unethical and . . . and . . . unconstitutional."

"Please," Ms. Giles said, a little impatient, "can we just do this tomorrow?"

But Darcy was getting mad and wasn't about to be put off at this point.

"God forbid the school should be embarrassed by letting a pregnant girl walk around," she said, patting her stomach for a little emphasis.

Suddenly there was fire in Ms. Giles's eyes as she glared at Darcy and said, "I don't give a damn if the school gets embarrassed. Look, I could get fired for this. The school's not asking you to drop out. I am."

"You?" Darcy said, not understanding.

Ms. Giles sighed and then spelled it out: "Look, Darcy. This is a small town. You're the editor of the school paper. You're popular. There are girls here who copy everything you do. I've seen it happen, Darcy. Pregnancy's contagious. Like suicide."

"Give me a break!" Darcy exclaimed. "I'm only having a baby!"

But Ms. Giles stayed serious.

"You know how many teenage girls get pregnant every week in this country?" she asked but didn't wait for Darcy to guess before she told her. "Twenty thousand."

"So I'm supposed to feel guilty if twenty thousand girls get knocked up?" Darcy said defensively.

"Nobody's asking you to save the world, Darcy. Just do the responsible thing." Ms. Giles waited a second, then let the serious set to her jaw warm into a smile as she put a hand on Darcy's arm. "Think about it."

Chapter 13

Darcy waited until she and Stan were doing their laundry in the Scrub-A-Dub-Dub that night before she told him about her session with Ms. Giles. She was pretty sure he wouldn't be too happy about her leaving school, but she wasn't prepared for how angry he got, and how suddenly. He was furious. Throughout practically the whole dry cycle he'd been stonily silent while she tried to make him see that this wasn't the end of the world.

"I thought it was horrible at first, too," she told him. "But after Giles explained it to me, I thought about it, and it's really not such a bad idea," Darcy said now, pulling their towels out of a dryer. The towels were bright chartreuse—the cheapest color at the carload sale they'd gone to for their linens. They clashed perfectly with the orange sheets they'd gotten at the same sale.

Stan slammed the door shut on the empty dryer and shouted over the whirring and sloshing of machines, "They can't make you quit! We could sue them."

"They're not making me do anything," Darcy said in what she hoped was the calm voice of extreme reasonableness.

"It still stinks, just suggesting it, and it sounds like Giles did more than just *suggest*."

Darcy just shrugged, trying to seem blasé.

"It was getting weird around there, anyway," she said, thinking of how humiliated she'd felt overhearing herself discussed in the girls' john—especially by Michaela and Elaine, whom she'd always dismissed as two girls going nowhere. That they were now in a position to put her down really upset her. She'd never told Stan about that conversation, but it was one of the big factors in her decision. "I'm going to night school."

Stan turned and looked up suddenly, a pair of jockey shorts in one hand, a dish towel in the other. "What do you mean, night school?"

Darcy figured she might as well give him both barrels at once. "I'm going to night school, *and* I'm getting a job."

"Oh, no," Stan shouted loud enough for two women to look up from their magazines. "*My* wife is not getting any job."

Darcy stared at him, put a hand on her hip, and said, "Good, Stan. You sound just like Fred Flintstone."

The one major feature of night school that Darcy overlooked was that it was at *night*. Pregnancy seemed to make her so much more tired than usual, and she'd been going to bed as early as eight o'clock a lot of the time. Going to school from seven to ten was going to be no mean feat.

She came down the hall the first night, found the door marked KENOSHA NIGHT SCHOOL—GRADES 10–12, and pushed it open.

She found herself facing a sea of unfamiliar faces of all races and ethnic groups. Most of them were adults, which was another thing she hadn't expected. She could feel disapproval in several of the gazes as she came in. At first she was embarrassed, a little ashamed, then she got angry.

They don't even know who I am, she thought. All

they see is "teenage mother" and think what a big tragedy. I'm just a statistic to them. One of the twenty thousand. Her anger made her feel a little braver as she approached the teacher's desk.

"I'm Darcy Elliot . . . uh, Ms. Giles called you? From Kenosha High?"

"Oh, yes," the teacher said. "I was expecting you. Class, we have a new student. Please say hello to Darcy."

In an amazing variety of accents, everyone chimed in with "Hello, Darcy." She felt like all eyes were on her and grew extremely uncomfortable. Then—to her surprise and relief—she saw two pregnant girls. They stood up in the back of the room and beckoned to her.

"Hey, Darcy," one called out.

"There's a seat back here," the other said.

She made a beeline for them.

"How far along are you?" one of them whispered to her as she sat down.

"Halfway through senior year," Darcy said.

"No . . . no, I mean . . ." the girl stammered, then, to show what she meant, she pointed at Darcy's stomach. Darcy slapped her forehead at her thickheadedness and laughed at herself, and told the girl, "Six months."

The next few weeks were a gray, wintery blur for Darcy. Studying and night school and afternoons working at Quickie Nickie's, where she had to wear a polyester Quickie Nickie maternity uniform (which they actually had in stock!). And put up with being harassed constantly by the manager, Fred Hudson—an incredibly nerdy guy who was a year behind her at Kenosha High. And politely change the burger orders of the snotty teenagers who were about the only customers in Quickie Nickie's. Why, Darcy wondered, did she suddenly see teenagers as another population? Why did she suddenly feel about a million years older than everybody else her age?

Worst of all was the time Darcy came through the parking lot, lugging a huge bag of garbage to the dumpster, already miserable, only to hear Michaela shout out the window of her car, "Hey, Darcy! That what you're wearing to the prom?"

This was followed by the roar of laughter from the other girls in the car as it peeled out of the lot, and by the tears that flowed out of Darcy's eyes and froze to her cheeks.

One chilly afternoon in early April, when Darcy was sitting up in the apartment, as close as possible to the heat vent (which now had old pantyhose stretched over it as a lint catcher), studying for a calculus midterm, the door buzzer went off. She looked down the stairs to see a surprise visitor—Stan's mother!

"Mrs. Bobrucz!" she exclaimed. "Come on up."

After taking off her old tweed coat and babushka scarf, Mrs. Bobrucz made a slow tour of the apartment.

"I stitched this," she said, fingering the material of the tent.

"I know," Darcy said. "Stan told me. Now it's our bathroom."

Mrs. Bobrucz peeked inside and giggled.

"So it is."

"Would you like some coffee?" Darcy said, wondering why—after all this time—Stan's mother was suddenly here for a little visit.

"Oh, don't go to any trouble," Mrs. Bobrucz said. It was what she said whenever you offered her anything.

"I already have a pot made up," Darcy assured her. "Do you take milk or sugar?"

"No, just black."

"Me, too," Darcy said, pouring out two mugs of coffee, wondering silently when the reason for this visit was going to come out. And then it did. Stan's mother handed her an envelope.

"This came for Stan," she said. "I think it's about his scholarship."

Darcy looked at the envelope so long it became awkward. Mrs. Bobrucz tried to change the subject—and the mood.

"Really good coffee, Darcy."

"Thanks. It's French roast. I put in a little cinnamon, too."

"Does Stan drink coffee now?"

"Mmmhmm."

"Boy, everybody's changed so much!"

"Not really," Darcy said. "He's still the same. He should be home in a bit. Why don't you wait?"

Suddenly Mrs. Bobrucz got all nervous, set her coffee mug down, and started fiddling with her gloves.

"Oh, no," she said. "I've got to go. Vic'd kill me if he knew I was here."

And with that, she got up to leave. When she was halfway to the door, she turned, and in a less friendly tone of voice said, "By the way . . . Vic knows about your marriage. He says you forged something, that with one phone call he could have you both put in jail."

"Mrs. Bobrucz," Darcy said, going over and putting a hand on her mother-in-law's shoulder, "this isn't like you, talking about putting me and Stan in jail. What's really bothering you?"

"You should've invited your mother to that wedding."

"She hates what I'm doing."

"I can understand you not inviting Vic . . . and *me*. But your own mother." Darcy could see that Stan's mother was about to cry, and suddenly she understood that it was herself she was really talking about. She was upset that *she* hadn't been invited.

"We really wanted you there. But we were afraid Mr. Bobrucz and my mother would try to stop us if they knew."

Stan's mother wiped her eyes with a Kleenex that she pulled from her coat pocket and admitted, "I suppose they would have. You poor babies." She stopped here and looked like she had something else on her mind. Finally she asked, "You wouldn't happen to have any pictures, would you?"

Darcy laughed, flattered in a funny way.

"Oh, yeah. Sure. Of course, it wasn't the kind of wedding you see in magazines or anything." She went over to her desk and pulled out a small stack of terrible, out-of-focus snapshots and handed them to Mrs. Bobrucz.

"Who cares if it wasn't high society?" she said. "Every wedding is beautiful in its own way."

She was a great audience for the photos. She oohed and aahed and looked practically forever at each picture.

"Oh, your dress is so pretty. Stan looks so grown up. Who's the Oriental gentleman?"

Darcy looked down at the letter from Cal Tech she was still holding. Stan's mother saw this and read her thoughts.

"You think he'll go if he gets the scholarship?" she asked Darcy.

All Darcy could do was shrug. She really didn't

know. She didn't even know what *she* wanted him to do, if this envelope was the scholarship offer—which it probably was. On the one hand, she didn't want him to be stopped in any way from fulfilling his dreams. On the other hand, it was pretty hard to imagine him going to college—at least full time—with a baby to support.

He came home later that night after he got off at Kolby's.

"Darcy?" he shouted on his way in.

"I'm in the john," Darcy called from the tent. She could hear him dumping his books on her desk and knew he'd spotted the letter. She popped her head up through the tent's skylight.

"What's it say?" she asked.

He didn't answer. She flushed the toilet and came out of the tent just as he was crumpling the letter and throwing it out the window into the snow-covered dumpster below.

"What're you doing?" she said.

"I didn't want the damn thing, anyway," he said.

"You didn't get it?" she said.

"It would've just screwed everything up," he said.

He's so strong in the face of rejection, Darcy thought.

She came over and wrapped her arms around him and held him tight.

"I think it *would* have screwed things up," she was free to admit now. "Still, you'd have felt better if *you'd* turned *them* down."

"No I wouldn't," he said.

"You are the world's worst liar," she said and hugged him as close as her present condition would allow. The two of them stood there, in the warmth of the apartment, while just outside, on top of all the other debris filling the dumpster, rested a crumpled letter which started:

> Dear Mr. Bobrucz:
> Congratulations! You have been awarded a Chandler Foundation Scholarship. Your tuition and dormitory lodging will be provided . . .

Chapter 14

April turned to May—a month that started off bleakly for Darcy.

The first low point was losing her job at Quickie Nickie's. By this time, she was so pregnant she could barely *see* past her stomach, much less reach around it. One day when the buzzer went off on the French fryer, all she could do was flap around like Flipper—trying futilely to get to the Off button, while Fred Hudson just stood smugly behind her with his arms folded across his chest, smirking.

He crooked his finger at Darcy, beckoning her into his office. She knew precisely what he was going to say. She turned to Henry, another Quickie Nickie employee, and told him, "I cannot stand to be fired from a burger joint this low on the scale. I could stand being fired from McDonald's or Burger King, but not from Quickie Nickie's."

So she turned back to Fred and shouted—loud enough to be heard through the entire restaurant, "I quit—on ethical grounds! I refuse to work in an establishment where the beef does *not* come from cows." She left it at that, letting the next question dangle in everyone's mind as she stalked out into the world of unemployment.

Her stalking only carried her as far as out the door. From there, Darcy lost her bravado, grew increasingly depressed, and trudged home—oblivious to the perfect spring day around her.

More and more, lately, she felt detached from the larger world around her. She'd lost touch with most of her old friends from school. Today, free from Quickie Nickie's, she thought, I'll fix that. I'll call Lila. Get together with her and Marnie.

But Lila's phone just rang and rang when she tried calling. Same with Marnie's. Then it came to her—like the little light bulb over the cartoon character's head.

"They're in school," she said aloud to herself, then waited until late afternoon to try again. She got hold of Lila around four.

"Hey," she said, "it's me."

"Darcy! I was just going to call you for a little chat. I was making myself finish my calculus homework first. You were going to be my treat."

"What I was thinking is that you could be *my* treat," Darcy said. "How about coming with me tomorrow? I'm going to scour the resale shops, try to find a chest of drawers for the youngun."

"Oh, hon, I'd love to. But I promised Marnie I'd go roller-skating with her and Lyn and Sharon and Cindy. You know."

Darcy knew all right. Her old crowd. And she couldn't even be hurt that they hadn't asked her. How could they? How was an eight-and-a-half-month-pregnant person going to roller-skate? Eight-and-a-half-month-pregnant persons stayed home and knitted and waited. Alone, it seemed.

"Oh, guess what?" Lila said, to change the subject probably.

"What?"

"You're not going to believe this—but I got nominated for prom court."

"You what?" Darcy blurted out before she could stop herself. The prom court was so mindless, so adolescent.

"Oh, well, you know I don't take it seriously," Lila said defensively. "It's just a kick." But Darcy could hear in her voice that she was a little hurt. Usually the two of them were perfectly in sync—they liked the same things and people, and made fun of the same stuff. If she and Lila were growing apart, it was serious. And it was probably her fault.

But what could she do about it, really? She was a married woman now with a baby on the way. She had an overworked husband and a lot of hard financial realities. How could she be expected to get into conversations about who was going together and who'd asked whom to the movies and who'd made the prom court?

When she got to the end of this bunch of thoughts, Darcy realized that while she'd been thinking them, an awkward silence had been building on the line. Lila misinterpreted this as hurt feelings on Darcy's part and tried to smooth things over.

"Hey! I know," she said. "Why don't you come over to the roller rink with us tonight? Just hang out and watch. You can be our chaperone or something."

Even though she knew Lila was just trying to lighten up the conversation, she'd inadvertently hit a sensitive chord. *Chaperone*. Someone older and out of the running. It was one of those moments when Darcy was thankful that television-phones had never caught on. She couldn't have stood for Lila to see the tears that were running down her cheeks as she said flatly, "Oh, no thanks," and hung up.

It was clear that her old friends were all busy, in another place. And Darcy was here. Alone.

She was still alienated from her mother, from

Stan's family, and isolated even from Stan. During this time that they'd both had jobs and been going to different schools, they hardly had an hour together a day. And if they did, it was usually just before bed, when Darcy ws so exhausted she was bleary.

She and Stan used to talk about everything—ideas, their future. Now the future had become focused on the baby, and the present consisted of just getting through each day, keeping up with their schoolwork, coming up with enough money to pay the important bills—gas, light, rent, phone.

At least Stan still had some contact with the old crowd. But while Darcy felt good about this in one way, it worried her in another. "Contact" could mean more than just talking and hanging out. And "the old crowd" did include people like Michaela—who were very attractive, very available, not bogged down with a million financial worries, and not eight-and-a-half-months pregnant.

As she heaved up the long flight of stairs to the apartment, Darcy tried to think of something she could do to cheer herself up. By the time Stan got home, she'd found it.

"Wilma?" he shouted up the stairs. "I'm home. It's Fred . . . Fred Flintstone."

When he came through the door, his mouth and eyes opened wide in disbelief.

"Why'd you do—that?" he said.

Suddenly Darcy became self-conscious. She was sitting in front of a propped-up mirror, a pair of scissors in her hand, and was nearly finished with an extremely semiprofessional haircut. She looked in the mirror again. It *was* pretty shocking. She'd had long hair since forever. She looked down at the newspapers spread under her chair and saw all the huge clumps of red hair. In a weird way, it was like a part of her past was lying there at her feet.

"Why?" Stan repeated.

"Well, I tried on my dress for the prom," Darcy said, trying to simplify all the emotions that had been whirling through her today, "and I look like a parade float." She gestured toward the bed, where the dress—a huge pile of ruffles—had been crumpled up and discarded.

"I also itch everywhere, and my ankles are fat, and I've been working on the same article for two weeks, and I got fired from Quickie Nickie's."

"No!" Stan said in mock disbelief. "I'm impressed. I don't think they've ever fired anyone. You might be able to get into the *Guinness Book of Records*."

Then he came over and knelt beside where she was sitting and said, "I hate to tell you this, but there's something else."

"What?" Darcy said.

"Your feet. There's something missing."

She looked down at her bare feet. What else could be wrong with her? But then Stan pulled a shoe box out of the bag he had with him. And from the box he pulled a shimmering dance slipper. It really was beautiful.

"For the prom," he said.

"Oh, Stan," she wailed, "I'm not going to the prom. They'd have to rent a bigger gymnasium if I came!"

He ignored her and started to slip the shoe onto her foot.

"If this fits, you're going to have to give all this up," he said and gestured with a sweep that took in the whole dismal apartment. "You'll have to move to the castle with me and live happily ever after."

She had to laugh. Of course, the shoe fit perfectly.

She let him put the other one on, then stood up to admire them.

"So?" Stan asked her. "What do you think?"

"I don't know," Darcy said, trying to peer over her belly, not knowing whether to laugh or cry. "I can't see them."

"I can," Stan said.

"And?"

"Perfect. Just like you," he said, looking at her with such a look of love that she almost felt it, like a wave.

Darcy *did* go to the prom—in spite of the fact that she was due to have the baby any second now. And that she was so pregnant that no dress could hide it. And that she could barely balance herself on the beautiful sequined slippers.

Still, she gamely marched through the parking lot toward the gym, using Stan's arm for support—both emotional and physical.

"Love your hair!" someone shouted from across the lot. It was Michaela, of course. "It's so French!" she added sarcastically. Darcy self-consciously reached around and felt the prickly ends where there used to be hair.

Chris, Marnie, Lila, Ron, Retro, and the rest of the old crowd were hanging out around the entrance to the gym. Dressed up for the prom, they all looked so different. For a moment, Darcy didn't feel so conspicuous. If everyone looked odd tonight, maybe she didn't stand out that much, after all.

"Hey, Bobrucz!" Chris said. "Remember, the tux turns into a pumpkin at midnight!" He had snuck it out of his father's rental shop so that Stan could have something to wear tonight. Stan gave him an appreciative thumbs-up sign, and said, "I owe you one!"

They were now at the entrance to the gym. Music and revolving colored lights were pouring out.

"Oh, Stan," Darcy moaned quietly, "it took me ten minutes just to get out of the car. How am I going to make it out onto the dance floor?"

"Simple," Stan said in a matter-of-fact voice. "I rented a forklift."

"You think of everything," Darcy said.

Off to the side, in what was usually the gym corridor, someone had built a little set for prom photos—a white trellis covered with terrible plastic morning glories.

"If you two will just stand on the white tape," the hired photographer said, motioning them over, "we can capture this memory forever. Good. Good. Yes, right there."

As he got behind his camera, Darcy whispered to Stan, "I can really do this, right? I can—"

But she was cut off by a purring voice from behind them. "Pretty foxy in a tux, boy."

Michaela again. Trouble. Both Darcy and Stan looked away from the camera and saw her hanging by the door in a knock-out black strapless gown. She was with a date, but her attention was clearly on Stan. She stared at him so long it was a little embarrassing for everyone else around. Finally she managed to acknowledge Darcy's presence, too.

"Hi, stranger."

"Hi, Michaela," Darcy said in a tone of voice she hoped conveyed the message, *Go jump in the lake*.

"I haven't seen you in . . ." Michaela began, then stopped and remarked, "Oh boy, you are *huge!*"

As Darcy responded with a frozen, mortified, humiliated smile of despair, the flash went off.

"There!" said the photographer, oblivious to the situation. "Memories are made of this!"

"I can't," Darcy told Stan when he suggested they go into the gym and dance. "I just can't."

Instead of trying to persuade her, he just nodded. One of the really great things about Stan was that he usually understood, and on the first beat.

"I've got an idea," he said and led her by the hand down the hall, through a door marked DO NOT ENTER, up a narrow flight of stairs, and out onto the rooftop of Kenosha High.

"Wow!" Darcy said, looking around at the lights of the city. "I didn't even know you could get up here. How'd . . . ?"

"You can't put a DO NOT ENTER sign in front of a teenage guy. It's like putting cheese in front of a mouse."

It was really an ugly rooftop, with a tar surface interrupted by heating vents. But for tonight, for Stan and Darcy, it was the most romantic place in the world. High above the muffled sounds of talk and laughter from the prom below, listening to the muted strains of Sam Cooke's "You Send Me," they danced slowly at a private prom of their own.

"I just love a guy who knows how to rescue a girl," Darcy said, kissing Stan on the nose. "Except up here you can't really show your stuff." Stan was one of the best dancers in the school.

"Who says?" he challenged, getting Darcy in a tango grip as though preparing to sweep her off her feet. "We can show the lady something light and breezy." He took her hand and spun her out from him.

Darcy squealed with delight, laughing, trying to

keep her balance as he spun her back in toward him.

"Or we can do this slow and sexy," he said, trying to pull her in close to him. Both of them cracked up as they tried to find a way to be close with Darcy's stomach in between. Finally, they found a kind-of fit.

"Ah, there," Darcy said with a sigh.

"And now..." Stan announced, "...now for the famous Bobrucz dip—known to leave women..."

"...on the floor," Darcy said, groaning with sarcasm as he lowered her to the floor. Then she began groaning in a different way. Stan pulled her up nervously.

"What's the matter?" he asked. "It's happening, isn't it?"

"I'm not sure," Darcy said, a little stunned. "But I'm wet, down there."

Stan looked down at the rooftop where they stood.

"Your water broke," he said. "Just like it said in the book. I'm getting us to the hospital!"

He took his tux jacket and draped it around her shoulders as he led her down from the roof. Suddenly Darcy had another contraction. She took a deep breath, then looked at him with plaintive eyes, and said, "Where's the forklift?"

Chapter 15

By the eighth hour of labor, Darcy felt like she'd been through a war. And it wasn't over yet. The contractions that had started up on the school roof had kept on coming, were still coming, but so far—no baby.

Stan was exhausted, too. He'd hardly left her side for a minute the whole time. Sometimes she appreciated him being there. But there were periods when she felt so awful or so punchy in the aftermath of a bad contraction that she couldn't have cared less that he was there. And—in the middle of the worst of the pain—she actively wished he'd go away. On a vacation to the Himalayas. And in the worst of those worst moments, she hated him—for getting her into this in the first place, and for not having to go through any of this agony now.

At this particular moment—a lull—she was grateful he was there.

"Oh-oh," she said. "Here comes another one."

"Do you want the tennis ball? The paint roller?" he asked, then, when she didn't answer, picked up the paint roller and massaged her tailbone with it as she clenched into the contraction, which was followed by an even stronger one.

"Water," Darcy gasped as the second contraction eased and she moved into the transition period. He put a flexi-straw into a Styrofoam cup and gently pushed the straw between her lips.

"Just pour it . . . on my head," she said pathetically, feeling completely whipped.

Stan filled an ice pack on the bedside table. The pain returned and her panting gave way to screams. He turned.

"Do the pattern breathing," he said, "like we practiced with the Lamaze book, okay?" He imitated it to coach her along.

"Forget the pattern breathing!" she screamed at him. "I want a painkiller!"

He started to rub her back again. He was dutifully going through all the husband-partner motions they'd learned from the book. Suddenly she hated him again. Why couldn't she be rubbing his back while *he* gave birth to this baby?

"Painkiller!" she shouted again. She realized she was throwing a tantrum. It was the only thing about the moment that felt good.

"The nurse went to check with the doc . . ." Stan said nervously.

"And don't *touch* me!" she shouted. "Don't you ever touch me again. I hope you had fun, Stan."

She could see she was shocking him. Good! He rushed to pick up his "Expectant Father" book and started flipping pages. When he found what he wanted, he read aloud, "The transition period. When she can turn on you like—"

"Was it fun? Huh? If I live to be a hundred, I'm never letting you take me camping again."

She knew she sounded like a maniac. She must have looked like one, too, because at this point Stan started backing away from her, saying, "Jeez. Chain Saw Massacre . . ." Then he turned and shouted out toward the hallway, "Nurse!"

Then, as suddenly as she had become enraged, her

anger washed away, replaced by pure pain and utter exhaustion. She reached out, took his hand, and said, "I can't take it, Stan. Please . . ."

She watched him lurch out of the room. At the door he bumped smack into the doctor, who was on his way in. She listened from inside her pain as Stan got angry for her.

"Do something, will you!" he shouted. "You're not taking care of her. She's my wife and she's . . ."

But the doctor didn't let him finish. He was intent on Darcy. He brushed past Stan, came over to the bed, and announced, ". . . and she's having her baby. Now!"

As they wheeled her out to the delivery room, Darcy heard another woman screaming from another labor room, "And if you ever come near me again, Anthony, you are a dead man!"

The next thing she knew, Darcy was on the delivery table, surrounded by equipment and masked faces. One of them was Stan's. She could tell by his eyes, which at the moment were small with worry. He stared hard at her, as if to say something, to put a message across this cold, clinical, scary space between them. But then the doctor was there, demanding her attention.

"Okay, now push down harder . . . a little harder," he said.

"I am," Darcy said. She couldn't push any harder than she was. What did they want from her?

"Push your baby down," the doctor was saying again. "And lean into it."

"I *am* pushing," Darcy said, feeling wimpy, like she wasn't up to whatever was expected of her here.

"Push harder. Push through the pain, Darcy." She recognized that voice as Stan's. Easy for him to say. And then suddenly it got worse, much worse.

"It's ripping!" she screamed. "It's burning!"

"It's crowning!" the doctor said. "Push now."

She did.

"That's it. Push again."

She did.

"That's it."

"You got it, Darcy. Come on!" Stan again. The cheerleader. She'd kill him when this was over. She was sick of the pain and sick of everyone telling her what to do. She gritted her teeth, felt her face go red, scrunched her eyes, and gave one giant push. That ought to make everybody happy.

And just like that, it happened. She felt the baby slide out, then, through eyes bleary with tears, saw the doctor hoist it in the air. Suddenly the delivery room was filled with the first wail of a new life.

"It's a girl!" Stan was shouting. "It's a girl!"

She supposed she should be feeling some big rush of maternal joy, but all Darcy felt was exhaustion. She watched the nurse suction mucus from the baby's nose and mouth, then lay her on Darcy's stomach. The doctor held the umbilical cord and offered Stan a pair of scissors.

"Would you like to cut the umbilical cord?" he asked.

"Uh," Stan said nervously, looking around, "don't you have someone a little more qualified?"

The nurse smiled and patted his shoulder, and then he did it. Then the nurse wrapped the baby in a blanket and handed her to Stan. Darcy could see that he was astounded, awed. He held the baby out to her.

"Want to see your beautiful baby girl?"

"She's nice" was about the most enthusiastic thing Darcy could think of to say. Then, in a quiet voice, she told him, "I want my mother, Stan. Go get her, please."

And then she rolled over to face the wall.

Chapter 16

Darcy's mother stepped briskly off the elevator when it reached the maternity floor. With her was a caseworker from the county adoption agency.

"If you could just talk to her calmly, be sensitive," Darcy's mother urged the woman, "I'm sure she'll come around. And then, that's that."

"Mrs. Elliot,' I've been an adoption liaison for ten years. If your daughter decides to give the child up, she has six months to change her mind."

Darcy's mother smiled. "She'll be in Paris by then. And after that, college. This will all be in the distant, blurry past."

As they rounded a corner of the hallway, they saw a nurse carrying a blanket-wrapped bundle of baby, on her way to some waiting mother.

"Oh, excuse me," Mrs. Eliot said. "I'm looking for my daughter and her baby. Darcy Elliot."

The nurse was clearly searching her mind and not coming up with "Elliot." Finally Mrs. Elliot remembered.

"I'm sorry. Maybe it's under Bobrucz."

The nurse smiled slowly. "Well, if it's Bobruczes you're looking for—your son-in-law went home to get some sleep, your daughter's right up here in room 507, and this"—she unfolded the blanket to reveal a baby sleeping with tiny fists curled up by its mouth —"this is your granddaughter."

Mrs. Elliot looked down at the tiny, sleeping face

and completely and totally melted. She tried to speak.

"I . . . uh . . . I-I-I . . . yaghhh . . ."

The adoption official put a hand lightly on Mrs. Elliot's shoulder.

"We lose a lot of them this way," she admitted as she turned to go.

Darcy was lying on her side, curled up in her hospital bed—a little like a baby herself. She heard someone come into the room. Probably another nurse. But she could feel that the visitor was not moving or leaving, just standing there behind her. She turned over. It was her mother, glowing and so happy. And the first thing she said was, "She's beautiful."

Who? Darcy thought for a second. Then—*Oh, of course. The baby.* As far as Darcy was concerned, everyone was paying an awful lot of attention to the baby. But then her mother reached out and began stroking Darcy's forehead, an old-timey thing she used to do when Darcy was upset. It was just what she needed now.

"I don't know why this didn't come to me before . . ." Darcy's mother was saying. For a moment, Darcy thought it was the start of an apology. Great. She deserved one. But then her mother went on: "We can all go to Paris together."

Darcy opened her eyes slowly. Maybe she'd heard wrong. She'd been pretty groggy since the delivery. She opened her eyes wide and focused intently on her mother. But she really was saying, "Europeans are absolutely wonderful with babies. You can bring them to restaurants, movies . . ."

"Mom . . ." Darcy tried to stop this line of conversation, but she was too weak at the moment, her mother already on a roll.

"We can stay in some quaint little hotel. Order up room service and . . ."

Darcy worked herself up onto her elbows and reached out to put a hand on her mother's.

"Mom, forget this trip idea, okay? Stan has to work and—"

"Stan?" her mother said, clearly quite surprised at the notion. "Who said anything about Stan? I meant you and me and the baby. Three generations of Elliot women . . ."

Even though she was still extremely shaky, Darcy managed to sit up—propelled by disbelief, frustration, and hurt that her mother had so little understanding of who she was and where she was.

"But I'm married," she said, exasperated. "Stan's my . . . Why can't you just be my mother? Why can't you just crawl into bed with me right now—and put your arms around me . . ."

Her mother nodded and started to turn down the blanket and climb into the bed. But Darcy stopped her first.

"Just don't be my friend, okay?"

"But I am your—" Mrs. Elliot protested.

"No!" Darcy said, almost shouting. "I don't want that. It comes with all these . . . these strings! When you're a mother, you just love somebody. That's it!"

Then, exhausted and frustrated, Darcy crashed back onto the bed, rolled over to face the wall, and pulled the sheet up over her head.

"Leave me alone," she told her mother in a small voice. "I don't want to be . . . your friend."

The next few days were a round of nurses taking her blood and temperature. Stan bringing flowers, friends visiting—none of which Darcy cared anything about. At first, she had just felt exhausted, like she'd run a marathon, twice. But even when her body started healing and she could feel strength seeping back, her mind stayed flat, her thoughts gray. Jokes didn't strike her as particularly funny: the gossip her friends brought seemed boring. The food trays the nurses brought in looked totally unappetizing. Mostly, Darcy just watched the TV hooked up near the ceiling at the foot of the bed. TV was good; she didn't have to relate to it. She could watch the characters on the shows go through their shallow dilemmas as though they were being beamed in from another planet.

The most troublesome moments in the hospital were when they brought the baby in for her feedings. It just made Darcy feel confused and guilty. She knew she should be feeling something deep and special for this little creature, but she just didn't. She didn't think she was an especially cute baby—kind of red-faced and squinty-eyed really. Nor did she look particularly like either Stan or herself. She didn't do anything interesting—just ate, slept, and dirtied a diaper about every ten minutes.

"What should we name her?" Stan had asked excitedly the day after she was born.

"I don't care," Darcy had said, and then went back to "The Young and the Restless." She could feel Stan's eyes lingering on her in disbelief, but she didn't really care. She didn't really care about anything now. Let Stan do the worrying.

He was plenty worried when they checked out of the hospital. The computer in the bookkeeping office just kept rolling paper off the computer, sputtering as it kept printing out charges.

"Uh, excuse me," shouted Stan, who was holding the baby. "We only had *one*."

The bookkeeper was not amused. She remained stony-faced until the machine stopped. Then she ripped off the printouts, folded them up, and handed them to Stan. He flipped through until he got to the bottom line.

"Seven hundred and fifty dollars!" He gulped. "But we're on the payment plan."

"Those are extras," she said. Then, as Stan looked at the seemingly endless list, the computer began sputtering again and the bookkeeper looked over. "Oh, wait. There's more."

While she went to get the additions, Stan turned around and shrugged helplessly across the waiting room at Darcy, who was sitting lethargically in a wheelchair, attended by a nurse. He went over with the baby.

"Sure you don't want to hold her?" Stan asked.

"That's okay," Darcy said listlessly. She didn't want to hold anybody. She just wanted to go home and get in bed and curl up in front of the TV. She watched Stan give her a concerned glance. He gave her a lot of concerned glances lately. Well, too bad. He should have given her a concerned glance that morning on the camping trip. Then she wouldn't be in this position now. At the moment, she was also unhappy with him for naming the baby.

"How could you name a baby Theodocia? Couldn't you find something you like from *this* century?"

"I named her after my grandmother, okay?" he said defensively.

"Theodocia," Darcy mused. "Sounds like a Greek fishing boat. Or a crater on the moon."

"Look," he snapped, "they needed a name for the birth certificate. I asked you what you wanted . . . Look, call her anything you want. I don't care. Just call her something!"

"Oh, Mr. Bobrucz?" the bookkeeper called from across the room. He went back to the desk to pick up the last of the charge printouts.

"Extra extras," the bookkeeper said with a plastic smile. "How are you kids going to be paying for this?"

"Very slowly," Stan said dejectedly.

Chapter 17

"And a big welcome for our new contestant, Benjamin Harrison!" the hearty host on the game show was saying. "Any relation to our former president, Mr. Harrison?"

Darcy was lying on her side, on the double bed up in the apartment, watching the TV—which was also lying on its side. All their friends had come by to see the baby and visit. She wasn't interested. She knew they were curious and worried that she wasn't interested, but that didn't interest her either. Still, she couldn't help overhear them all talking across the room, in the kitchen, where Stan was holding Thea while Lila fixed her a bottle.

"Is Darcy breastfeeding her?" Chris asked. He'd read a book on babies and childcare, to keep up with what Stan was going through. This one book had made him an expert.

Darcy saw Stan shake his head and say, "She doesn't even want to hold the baby."

Lila handed him the warm bottle, and he slipped the nipple into the baby's mouth. "The doctor called it 'postpartum depression,'" he went on. "It has something to do with her age, all the changes. Hormones, I guess."

"The natural tendency to mother will kick in," Chris the expert reassured Stan. "It's a genetic animal instinct."

"What?" Retro piped up. "Like 'Wild Kingdom'?"

"Uh, sort of." Chris humored him.

"I don't know," Retro said, in what for him was "thoughtful mode." "Maybe she didn't get enough oxygen to her brain during the delivery."

"Maybe she wanted a boy," Stan said.

"You know," Retro offered informatively, "in China, they only allow one kid per family, so sometimes, if they have a girl first . . . they kill it."

Darcy watched from a distance as Chris slugged Retro in the arm. Retro really ought to have his own TV show, she thought. Then she heard Lila offer Stan *her* psychological analysis of the situation.

"Look, this is a complex manifestation of jealousy. You're paying too much attention to the 'other woman.'"

Stan just looked bewildered in the face of this concept.

"I didn't know you could pay too much attention to a baby," he said as the door buzzer went off.

Darcy contemplated this exchange as if she were watching it on one of her soaps, as if the conversation were between two characters talking about another character.

Still holding the baby, Stan went to see who was at the door. It was his mother and his sister Mary—coming to see Thea for the first time. Mrs. Bobrucz kissed Stan and then grabbed the baby. Instant grandmother.

"Oh, just look at her! Oh, there she is. Oh, look at that eeny weeny face!"

"Does Dad know you're here?" Stan asked.

"Are you kidding?" his mother said to him, as though he must be out of his mind. Then she went back to her new, greatest interest in life. "Oh, and look at those eeny weeny feet!"

Mary, always the curious one, asked Stan, "Where's Darcy?"

"Over there. In the bedroom," he said, pointing toward the bed, where Darcy appeared to be transfixed by the TV.

Mary studied the situation for a long moment, then —with all the expertise she'd accumulated from watching Phil Donahue and Oprah Winfrey and Dr. Ruth—gave her diagnosis:

"Postpartum depression."

Stan's father had refused to come and see the baby and had refused to let his wife see her either. But when Mary and Mrs. Bobrucz came back, he knew where they'd been. Both of them had baby love written all over their faces.

He played dumb, though, and just kept working out in his garden. His rose bushes were beginning to bloom. He loved roses—a gentle side to his rough character.

After a while, Mary came wandering out and started grilling him with questions.

"Dad?"

"Yeah?"

"Did Stan and Darcy name the baby after Grandma?"

He examined a tiny bud, holding it delicately in his large, dirty hand.

"I don't know."

An unsatisfactory answer as far as Mary was concerned. She moved on to the next question.

"Well . . . where did Grandma get *her* name?"

"From *her* mother. My grandmother Theodocia." He held out a hand, indicating he wanted the trowel. Mary handed it to him.

"Was your grandmother nice?"

Mr. Bobrucz thought for a moment, and his expression softened with memory.

"Nice? She was the best. One time when I was just about your age, I broke a window at school. I guess my mother wasn't home . . . because the principal called my grandmother into his office . . ."

Mary loved stories about her father as a boy. It was so hard to imagine him as anything but a big, gruff man.

"Did you get in trouble?" she asked.

He smiled, as if recalling something that happened just yesterday.

"That's the thing of it. Not only did she pay for the window—she never told my father. Because if she had . . . well, I'd be walking around with a limp to this day." He looked over at his daughter. "See, that's the thing about grandparents, Mare. They love you so much . . . that when you do something wrong, they don't even see what's wrong about it."

Mary nodded, taking this all in, adding it to her file of "Life Info." This only left one small point to clear up on the subject.

"Dad? Are you a grandparent?" she asked.

For once, Mr. Bobrucz was at a loss for words. He just stood there looking at Mary with more emotions going around inside him than he could handle, much less express.

Chapter 18

"And our champion for a week in a row—Benjamin Harrison, fifty thousand dollars!" the announcer blared in his hearty voice.

"Way to go, Ben," Darcy responded in a listless voice from where she was lying on the bed.

Across the room, Stan was changing Thea on the kitchen counter. She was a mess. A dozen Wet Ones hadn't made a dent in the problem.

"She's a dirty girl," Stan said, chatting up the baby. "She's a stinky girl. We're talking *Guinness Book of Records* here. We've got to call out the fire department. We've got to hose this little girl down." Which is just what he did, using the spray attachment on the sink. Then he dried her off, popped a Pampers on her, and brought her over to Darcy.

"I'm late for work. Kolby's going to kill me," he said, trying to make himself heard over the screaming TV audience, which was going wild for Benjamin Harrison, who'd just won another ten thousand. "Keep an eye on her, okay?"

As soon as he put the baby down next to Darcy, he made a dash for the door. But he got stopped at the top of the stairs. He stuck his head back into the apartment and shouted, "Throw me the car keys, will you?"

Without looking, Darcy reached for the keys on the table next to the bed. She tossed them to Stan as Benjamin Harrison deliberated over a particularly hard question. She liked Benjamin Harrison. He seemed like a nice guy. Rich now, too.

Stan caught the keys and once again headed out the door. And once again stopped in his tracks.

"Oh, this is good," he said. "Great, Darcy." He held up a large key ring with pastel, oversized plastic keys. One of Thea's toys.

Darcy ignored him. She just stayed on the bed listening to him find his keys then bound down the stairs. She watched the rest of the quiz show, then a couple of soaps, and then turned off the TV. Suddenly, she was sick of watching the pale dramas of pale characters. Suddenly, she wanted to be back in her own life.

She jumped out of bed and took a shower and washed her hair. She put on a new robe Marnie had brought her in the hospital. Then she hauled out Lila's typewriter and set it up on the table. She rolled in a fresh white sheet of paper and began punching away at the keys. She was going to write her article on having the baby—real, true, first-person journalism.

When she was done with the first sentence, she leaned back in the chair and read it aloud:

"It's like when she was ripped from inside me, all the things I loved about being young . . . were ripped out, too."

She looked over at Thea, who was lying in the middle of the bed, her chubby little legs in the air. She was holding onto the plastic keys, gumming them and cooing and looking over at Darcy, who typed out, then read aloud, the next sentence of the article:

"Maybe if I could just learn to *understand* her."

She looked over at Thea again and this time stared too hard, for too long, which sent Thea into a wail of crying. With a sigh of exasperation, Darcy put her hand on the typewriter and waited to see if she'd have to go over and pick her up. But she stopped crying on her own. For a moment the apartment was utterly silent. And in that silence, Darcy could clearly hear shuffling sounds from behind her, outside the back windows, where the landing ran along the apartment.

She looked up and saw a shadowy figure moving slowly along the wall. Someone was definitely out there!

Very slowly, she got up and went to the phone and dialed 911. When a voice answered at the other end, she said, in a nervous whisper, "There's a man outside my back window. Oh, okay. 4653 North Vickers. Second floor, rear. Bobrucz. B-O-B . . . look, I'm about to be murdered. Wing it!"

She slammed down the phone and stood absolutely still. She could still hear the noises. She moved over the bed and scooped up the baby, who had started to cry again. She opened up her robe and tucked the baby inside. Instantly, the baby stopped crying and began making tiny sucking sounds. Darcy had to smile.

"You little devil," she said, opening the robe and peeking in to see Thea taking the opportunity to get a little milk. Darcy reached in and caressed the baby's head. She'd read some articles on nursing, and they'd said that it was an experience that brought mother and child closer together, but they hadn't given any real idea of the magnitude of the experience. Darcy was just floored with new feeling for her baby.

She looked toward the back windows and said in a voice sharp with protectiveness, "Look, go away! I called the cops. Besides, there isn't any money here. We just got the second notice on our light bill."

She thought she heard the footsteps scuffle off, but she couldn't go outside and check. The sensible thing seemed to just wait for the police to arrive. She went over to the bed and put Thea down and curled around her. She was now blissed out with sleep. Darcy watched her. She was so innocent looking and really kind of cute in her own way. Why hadn't she seen that before? And her hair definitely had a reddish tinge. And her ears were nearly exact miniatures of Stan's. Really, she was absolutely fascinating to look at. Darcy just got lost in her.

And then nearly went through the ceiling when, a few minutes later, there was a loud knock at the door.

A brusque man's voice thundered, "Mrs. Booblitz? Captain O'Connell here. Kenosha Police."

Darcy got up and moved tentatively toward the door, holding the baby.

"Yes?"

"We got the guy you called about. Caught him sneaking down the back way."

Darcy felt a huge wave of relief pass through her. She opened the door to find two burly cops standing there.

"I really apprecia—" she started to say, but one of the cops interrupted her.

"Only one problem, lady. The guy says he knows you."

And then the second cop yanked the intruder by the arm into the doorway. It was Stan's father, with a look on his face Darcy had never seen before—embarrassment.

"You want to press charges?" one of the cops asked.

"Oh, no. Thank you, officer." She closed the door and turned to Stan's dad.

"Hi, Darcy," he said sheepishly.

"Hi, Mr. Bobrucz."

"I was just going to sneak a peek from the back

window there. I didn't mean to scare you." He held up a brown paper bag. "I brought some fruit. So that's the baby, eh?"

"This is Thea."

"She's beautiful," he said in a soft voice she'd never heard him use before.

"Would you like to hold her?" Darcy asked.

"Okay . . ."

"Why don't you put your bag down?" she said, and when he had, she handed him his granddaughter. He peered at Thea's face.

"Look at that eeny weeny face. And those eeny weeny feet."

Darcy just stood by, enjoying the moment, kind of proud of her daughter. She seemed to be doing what no one else ever had—turning Mr. Bobrucz from a gruff guy into a complete mush heart. Now he looked up at Darcy.

"You named her after my grandmother. She would have liked that."

"It was Stan's idea, really," Darcy said. She wanted to make sure he got credit with his father.

"Are you going to tell him I was here?"

She nodded and said, "He's my husband. We don't have secrets."

"Well, I'll tell you one thing," Mr. Bobrucz said, looking down at Thea, clearly on his own grandpa track. "This kid's going to Cal Tech."

That night, Stan came in the door, beat, numbed out as usual after a long day at work. He looked over toward Thea's crib, then toward the bed, looking for her in the places Darcy usually left her, ignored.

She could see that, for an instant, he was afraid they weren't there. Then he looked over and spotted Darcy in the corner of the room, where she was sitting in the rocking chair, cradling Thea in her arms, breastfeeding her.

"Wow," he said, "what a beautiful sight."

"I'm not sure I have any milk left, but she seems to like it."

He came over and leaned down and kissed them both—mother and daughter.

"Your dad came by a little while ago," she said.

"What was *he* doing here?" Stan said, an edge coming sharply into his voice.

"He came to see the baby. He was very sweet, and Thea loved him."

"So did I when I was her age," Stan said bitterly.

Chapter 19

When Darcy lived with her mother, she and Lila used to spend their summer afternoons out in the backyard, lying at opposite ends of the old net hammock they'd string between two trees, their feet tangled up along with their talk and laughter.

This summer they had to find a substitute talking place—and one that could accommodate an extra—if extremely small—person. It was a bit of a comedown, but they kind of liked the bus bench in front of the Scrub-A-Dub-Dub. And the driver of the number 16 was getting to know not to stop for them. If he was in a good mood, he'd even wave as he went by.

Today they were just hanging out together more than actually talking. Lila was studying for finals while Darcy went through the classifieds scanning for another job.

"Hey," she said, "this is perfect. 'Big Bucks. Make Extra Cash in Spare Time. Easy-Going Sales.' I wonder if I could bring Thea along?"

She reached into her knapsack and pulled out what she thought was a pen, pulled the cap off with her teeth, and—just as she was about to circle the ad—got stopped by Lila, who was looking at her with slightly arched eyebrows.

"Hey, Darcy. That's Thea's thermometer."

Darcy grinned sheepishly and started digging through her sack for a real pen. Just then, Stan came running around the corner, full-tilt toward them.

When he got to the bench he said, "Hey, babe. Hey, Lila." And then scooped up Thea and held her over his head. "And here's Theezer!" He let the baby down and rocked her for a moment, then turned her around and held her nose to his.

"So what do you think about your old man, anyway?" he asked her. "Next week he's a high school graduate."

Thea responded by scrunching up her face.

"Don't look at me like that," Stan said, mock seriously. "If *I* have a future, kid—*you* have a future." Then he kissed her on the nose and handed her to Darcy.

"I'm late for my roofing job," he told her.

"Hey," she said, handing Thea back to him, "I've got night school. I thought that roofing job started next week."

"Yeah, well they want me to start early, and I don't want to blow this gig, Darcy," he said, handing the baby back to her.

"Well, I can't blow night school either," she told him.

They stared at each other for a long moment, then at the same time turned to Lila. She looked back at them, laughed at their helplessness, and held out her arms for Thea.

"Auntie Lila will read you a bedtime story," she said to the baby as Stan gave Lila's hair a tussle and Darcy gave her a kiss on the cheek.

When they'd both run off, Lila sighed and opened her textbook, propping it in front of Thea as though it were Mother Goose.

"Once upon a time," she began, "there was this weird thing called abnormal psych."

Two hours later, Stan stood bent over, pushing a

tar roller across a hot, flat roof. The fumes were stupifying, his clothes and shoes were ruined—covered with tar speckles—and he ached all over.

"This really is a terrible job," he said to the guy working next to him.

"Pays bad, too," the guy said and started laughing. And then the laughing sent him into a burst of wheezing. When he'd stopped, he said, "Steady work, though. I been at it thirty years."

Stan tried not to let his expression show how depressed this thought made him.

At the end of the week, Stan graduated from Kenosha High. Darcy sat with Thea on her lap, filled with pride for him. She knew that, of all the graduates filing up onstage, none had gone to greater lengths to get that diploma than her husband. She also had to admit he looked pretty cute in a cap and gown.

After the commencement ceremony, everyone mobbed out the front doors of the school. Darcy was talking with Chris, who'd given Thea his mortarboard to wear. It was about seven times too big for her, but she seemed to like wearing it and eating the tassle.

When she looked ahead to find Stan, Darcy saw that someone else had found him first. Michaela. Darcy overheard her hassling him.

"Oh, Stan, you're married . . . not *dead*. Ask her if you can go. Just *ask* her."

"Excuse me," Darcy said, stopping Michaela in her tracks by grabbing onto the wide sleeve of her graduation gown. "He doesn't have to ask me anything. This is a free country."

Michaela didn't dignify this with a reply. She just

stared at Darcy for a moment, then turned to Stan and said, "Looks like Mama said okay, boy."

"Michaela," Stan said, sounding extremely uncomfortable, "I don't . . ."

But she'd already linked her arm through his. Darcy felt anger spread through her like a flame. She glared at Michaela and said, "This time you're not getting my goldfish!" When Michaela didn't say anything in response to this, Darcy went on, to refresh her memory. "Fifth grade. Milton Krensky."

Michaela shrugged Darcy off. "You're so full of it."

"You remember Milton!" Darcy said, sure that Michaela did. "He gave me those two goldfish in the plastic bag. And you stole them out of my locker! It wasn't about Milton, or the goldfish. You didn't care about any of that. You just have to have what somebody else has!"

By this time, Darcy's voice had risen and a small crowd of kids had gathered, full of curiosity, wanting to be around if anybody started throwing punches. Michaela saw this and pulled deeper into her deep freeze of cool.

"If you'll excuse me," she said, looking at Darcy with an expression of total boredom. "I've got a party to go to."

But Darcy wasn't about to let her off the hook.

"The big challenge, right?" she hounded her. "And Stan's the biggest challenge . . . because he's got a wife and a kid who love him! Well, I'll tell you something, Michaela . . . and maybe you'd better take notes!"

She moved in, her face red, her expression intent, until she was almost nose to nose with Michaela. Then Darcy gave it to her.

"You're not just greedy . . . and selfish . . . and juvenile. You're stupid. Because if you spend your life grabbing at what everybody else has . . . you're going to end up with nothing!"

Chapter 20

When Stan came through the door of the apartment a few nights later, the whole place was dark, with candles flickering on the table.

"Ooooo," he guessed. "Someone's feeling romantic."

From the rocking chair, where she was sitting with Thea asleep in her arms, Darcy said in a flat, dead, defeated voice, "They cut off the electricity."

"They what?" he snapped and tore into the kitchen. He found the flashlight and started rummaging through the bill drawer until he found the red Final Notice from the electric company.

"Here it is," he said in his lecturing voice. She hated his lecturing voice. "Darcy, you don't take care of bills by stuffing them in a drawer."

"We couldn't pay them, Stan. What do you want me to do?"

He paced back and forth like Ralph Kramden on the old "Honeymooners" show. Was her life becoming like a TV sitcom? Darcy wondered. Is this what it's coming down to—a life constantly bogged down in small, hard, unsolvable problems?

"We're in deep trouble, Darcy," Stan went on as he continued to pace. "We're going to have to do some belt-tightening, that's all." He was moving from his lecturing voice into his gruff husband growl. Probably learned both from his father. His father! Now, there was a possible way out.

"Maybe we could ask your dad for a little help . . ." Darcy suggested casually.

"No way!" Stan snapped her sentence off in the middle. "We'll manage by ourselves. We'll do less entertaining."

"We don't do *any* entertaining—except sometimes I have Lila over on the bus bench. Do I have to cut that out?" But Stan was not about to be teased out of his mood. He was on a cost-cutting rampage through the apartment.

"Look, there's no reason we've got to have chocolate milk in the fridge . . . or French roast coffee—with cinnamon!"

Next he tore through the closet.

"And no more disposable diapers. What's wrong with cloth? Like my mom used on me! What's the—"

"Just stop, okay?" Darcy said, putting her hands over her ears. "Please. We barely have any costs. We're already down to the bare minimum. What we save on these little things won't even pay the light bill. So how are we going to pay for the big stuff—the real stuff?"

"What are you talking about?" Stan asked.

"College," Darcy said. "How are we ever going to pay for college?"

"College!" Stan shouted in total exasperation. "Open your eyes, Darcy. Forget college. We're not going!"

"How about next year, though?" Darcy said optimistically. "We can save up."

But Stan just looked at her with despair at the back of his eyes, then looked around the apartment hopelessly.

"We're going to be here the rest of our lives. I'm going to be a roofer and you . . . you'll go to beauty school."

Darcy could hear reality behind the deadness of his voice. It dawned on her that what he was saying was probably true.

"We're really not going, are we? We're not going anywhere."

"I am," he said roughly. "I'm going out for a beer."

He stomped toward the door in his heavy roofer's boots. Then, just before he got to the door, his macho exit was done in by a high-pitched squeak. Thea's rubber duck. Darcy was sure he'd see the humor in this, see that—awful as it was—they were in this together and had to stay together to work it out. She was sure he'd turn and grin that sweet, sleepy grin of his and walk back and take her in his arms.

But he didn't. He just kicked the duck into the corner and kept on going, out the door.

Thea woke up with the slamming of the door. Darcy nursed her, then gave her a bath, then took her outside to the bus bench, to get out of the dead heat of the apartment. When she'd been sitting there for half an hour, rocking Thea and singing some old rock-and-roll songs to her, Stan finally returned.

"Hi," he said softly, sitting down beside her on the bench.

They sat in silence for a few minutes, neither quite knowing what to say. When they finally did speak, it was in unison. "I'm sorry..."

They exchanged tentative smiles as Stan stood and took Darcy's hand. "Come on upstairs," she said, sighing with fatigue—both physical and emotional—as she rose. "I'll fix you dinner."

On the dark stairs on the way up, Stan stopped Darcy by putting a hand on her shoulder. Then he ran his fingers through her short hair.

"Do you think we'll ever make love again?" he asked her.

She was taken totally by surprise by the question. Having the baby had been so hard on her body. And since then, Thea's schedule—waking up crying to be fed at least once in the middle of every night—had her too dragged out to think romantic thoughts.

"Sure," she reassured him and smiled. "I just wish somebody would invent a way that you could sleep and make love at the same time."

They were halfway up the stairs, but both of them had the same idea simultaneously.

"If we're going to get physical again . . ." Stan said.

". . . this time we're going to be prepared!" Darcy finished his sentence.

So they turned around on the stairs and headed back down, and out, and over to the drugstore.

Darcy, holding onto Thea, filled Dr. Barrick's prescriptions for birth control pills *and* a diaphragm. While she was waiting, Stan went over and got two large boxes of condoms. Darcy thought for a moment, then picked up a box of contraceptive sponges. Stan added some spermicidal cream to the growing pile on the druggist's counter, and Darcy topped it with a package of Enko foam.

The druggist, returning, looked at this collection, then at Stan, Darcy, and Thea, and asked, "Kid been giving you a lot of trouble?"

About a week later, the subject of birth control came up again, but in an entirely different context.

Lila was baby-sitting Thea one night while Darcy was at night school. Class let out a little early and Darcy ran all the way home, thinking maybe she and

Lila could take the baby over to the 31 Flavors. She came up the stairs two at a time, then bounded through the door.

"Hey! I'm home!" she shouted to Lila.

Who sat up in bed with her boyfriend, Ron.

"Oh, I'm sorry," Darcy stammered, embarrassed. "I'll just take Thea for a walk."

But Ron was already hopping around, trying to get into his jeans and grab his shirt.

"No, no," he said nervously. "That's okay. Got to go. Bye, Darcy." To Lila, all he said was, "See you later."

Once he was out of the room, Darcy had a moment to think clearly, *and* to imagine the scene she'd just interrupted. She looked over at Thea. Asleep in her crib. Suddenly, Darcy went from being polite friend to protective mother.

"You did it . . . in front of my kid? Do you think she heard?"

"She was asleep," Lila said in a calming voice. "Look, it just happened."

"What do you mean, *It just* . . . You were baby-sitting!"

Darcy paced the room, confused and upset, then finally stopped and turned on Lila.

"When I left, you were sitting here," she said, pointing at the rocking chair. "And Ron was sitting over there," she said, indicating the daybed against the wall. She stopped for a long moment, then fixed Lila with a laser stare.

"You were using something, right?" she said in as calm a voice as she could come up with. "Just tell me you weren't dumb enough to . . ."

Lila looked off toward the kitchen. That she couldn't meet Darcy's eyes told her everything—everything she didn't want to hear.

"I told you, I didn't know this was going to happen," Lila said.

"You didn't *know!* Don't tell me you didn't *know*. You *know* everything. You *know* about cycles, and fallopian tubes, and zygotes for crying out loud. Look at me. You want a baby, huh? You want to feel like a thirty-year-old woman at seventeen?"

Darcy stopped and took a deep breath, trying to calm herself down. When she spoke, it was in a low voice. She pointed to the shelf over the sink.

"You were surrounded by an arsenal of contraceptives."

At this, Lila—usually the essence of cool and collected—burst into tears and blurted out, "It was my first time!"

"Your what?" said Darcy, incredulous. "But I thought . . ." Lila had told her she and Ron had been sleeping together for months. Now she just sat in the bed, clutching the sheet to her throat, looking sheepish.

"I only said I was doing it because you were doing it and I didn't want to . . . well, seem unsophisticated."

Darcy processed this information, then revealed to Lila, "But I said I was doing it with Stan because *you said* you were . . ."

Darcy collapsed onto the bed and the two of them held each other until they were laughing and crying at the same time. Finally Darcy fell backwards onto the mattress and said, "Ahhh! Life! It is so *strange* sometimes, eh, Li?" She reached over and grabbed something to wipe her nose with, oblivious to the fact that it was a Pampers. "I mean really just too damn strange . . ."

The two old friends looked at each other as their laughter died away and they exchanged a long silent look of knowing—that their lives were slipping and sliding around them, changing in ways they hadn't seen coming, and didn't really understand even now that they were happening.

Chapter 21

Darcy came in feeling hot and frazzled from her first day's work at a fast-food place even worse than Quickie Nickie's—the Pork Pit. She dug around in her shoulder bag for her mailbox key, even though she knew that all she'd probably find inside would be more bills.

"Hey!" someone shouted from the landing. It was Mrs. Kramer, the landlady. "Your kid's been crying all afternoon. Someone ought to turn you in—leaving your baby alone like that!"

"But I didn't leave her alone!" Darcy shouted in a panic. She'd left Thea with Stan. What was wrong? She raced up the stairs and, as she passed Mrs. Kramer, toward the sound of her baby squalling, the landlady said, "This is it. End of the month . . . you're out!"

Inside the apartment, Stan was flopped on the bed, clearly hung over, his arms wrapped around his head. Darcy tried to ignore him and rushed over to pick up the baby, who was red in the face from screaming.

"I fed her," Stan muttered from his cocoon. "I changed her. I rocked her. I tried everything."

"Maybe she's sick," Darcy said, pressing her palm to Thea's forehead. "Did you take her temperature?"

This got Stan out of bed. He went to the medicine cabinet and fumbled around, finally coming up with the thermometer.

"She's burning up, Stan," Darcy said, agitated. "I can feel it even without a thermometer." She shoved the baby into Stan's arms. "I said, *Feel her forehead!*"

"We have to call the doctor!" Stan said, suddenly snapping into his man-in-charge mode. "Immediately!"

Darcy grew calm, the kind of calm she only got down to when she felt truly insane and needed to put total control on herself. In a very flat voice she informed him, "We don't have a phone. We couldn't pay . . . our phone bill."

They both stared at each other, the baby between them—then rushed out the door and down the stairs.

Outside, they found a cab and got to the hospital. Thea turned out to just have the flu. While Stan talked with the nurse, Darcy used the phone in the emergency waiting room to make a call.

"Your little girl's fine," the nurse told Stan. "Doctor gave her a little shot of penicillin."

Darcy hung up the phone and came over to get the word from Stan.

"We can take her home tonight."

She nodded and then hesitated for a second, thinking of the most tactful way to phrase what she had to say.

"Here's the thing, Stan. I just talked to my mother." She sat down in one of the plastic chairs. "We're moving in with her."

Stan stood absorbing this for a moment, then plopped into the chair next to Darcy.

"That," he said, "is a truly terrible idea."

"You want to know something, Stan?" Darcy said, hopping out of her chair as soon as he'd slumped into his. "Right now, I really don't care *what* you think."

* * *

For some reason, Darcy thought moving back home would get her life more or less back to how it had been before. Instead of her and her mother having cinnamon coffee in the morning and French dinners and interesting conversations at night, she thought that now she and her mother and Stan would do these same thing.

This plan might have worked if only it hadn't been for two little problems—Stan and her mother. Her mother had always thought he was beneath Darcy, a working-class kid. Stan, on his part, just couldn't accept that he and Darcy were dependent on Mrs. Elliot for a roof over their heads. Sometimes, as much as Darcy loved him, she had to admit that Stan could be as pigheaded and macho as his father.

He would never, for instance—never *ever*—pull into a gas station to ask for directions. Nor would he concede that there might possibly be a jar top he couldn't unscrew. In the same way, he wanted to be king of his own castle. And this castle was already ruled by a queen.

By late August, they'd been living with Darcy's mother a few weeks. The days were hot and the nights not much cooler. Stan was sitting at the kitchen table having a late supper while Darcy fed Thea, who now sat in her own little chair that hooked onto the table.

The phone rang and Darcy went over to answer it while Stan just looked off into the middle distance—something he did a lot lately, especially after he'd had a few beers and was deep into brooding. He popped the top on another can now.

"It's Lila," Darcy told him now. "Everybody's going out to the lake. Want to go? She'll pick us up."

It was so hot and muggy and the air so still. The lake sounded great. Thea loved sitting on a blanket getting lots of attention, so they could just bring her along.

"I don't want to go," Stan said sullenly.

"Why not?" she prodded him. "It'll be fun. See everybody before they go off to school."

"You go. I don't want to."

Darcy thought for a moment of taking Thea and just leaving Stan home alone. But looking across the room, she could see how miserable he was, and she just didn't have the heart to run off and have fun without him. She took her hand off the receiver and told Lila, "No, I guess not. So say good-bye to everyone for us, okay? . . . You, too . . . Bye."

Just as Darcy was hanging up, they heard a car door slam. Darcy's mother.

"What's she doing here?" Stan said, irritated. "I thought she was at her French club."

"I thought so, too," Darcy said. Then, realizing that Stan only had on jeans, which her mother never thought was quite dressed enough, she urged him, "Put your shirt on. And please, don't start in with her tonight. It's too hot for an argument."

Mrs. Elliot breezed in, her arms full of packages.

"I'm home!" she said cheerily as she came through the door, then, looking at Darcy and Stan, added, "Oh, good, you're eating. I threw that old stew in the Crockpot this morning. How'd it turn out?"

"Magnifique," Stan said sarcastically.

Darcy gave him a look that read "don't start."

"You're so sweet. It's probably awful," said Mrs. Elliot, who either hadn't picked up on the sarcasm or was rising above it.

She pulled a bottle of wine out of a brown bag and

set it on the table in front of them, then put a corkscrew next to it.

"See, we don't have any rules around here," she said for Stan's benefit. Last night he'd told her he felt like he was in a straitjacket of rules and manners and schedules living around here.

Now she uncorked the wine and poured three glasses, saying, "And we drink wine with our dinner. Cabernet Sauvignon. Don't we, Darcy?"

She sipped the wine and smacked her lips a little to show she'd made a brilliant choice. Mrs. Elliot considered herself a wine connoisseur—in the under five-dollar-a-bottle range. She sat down with the two of them and paused a moment. Darcy knew her mother well enough to be pretty sure something was on her mind and that she was about to express it.

"Oh, I was thinking about what you said, Darcy."

What had she said? When? What was her mother talking about, Darcy wondered. She didn't have to wait long to find out.

"In the hospital. When I came to visit and you expressed your . . . your unhappiness with our relationship. I started thinking that there's really no reason I can't be your mother *and* your best friend."

"Mother, do we have to . . ." Darcy didn't particularly want to have this conversation, period. And she for sure didn't want to have it on a night when everyone was hot and cranky and when Stan had already had too much to drink and was just waiting for an opportunity to be rowdy and obstreperous. But her mother was on a roll, unstoppable.

"I approach everything as a learning experience." Then she turned to the baby. "We try to juggle all the roles, don't we, Thea?"

And with that she picked up a napkin and wiped the baby's mouth. Then she leaned over and wiped

Darcy's mouth. Stan took a look at this and walked out the back door with his beer in his hand.

When he'd gone, Mrs. Elliot turned to Darcy and said, "Well, maybe one rule." Her voice went cold as stone as she said, "I don't want any beer in this house."

Chapter 22

The next night, Stan and Darcy were up in what was now their bedroom, although they hadn't done anything to it, and it still looked like it had when Darcy had moved out. The walls were filled with team banners and rock posters, the bulletin board crammed full of souvenirs from dances and a hundred other memorable occasions—a leaf Stan had picked up on their first walk, Darcy's first story for the school newspaper. It didn't look like the bedroom of a married couple, but a married couple was on the bed. And they were talking in low voices so the wife's mother wouldn't hear.

"She's driving me crazy," Stan said, moaning for emphasis.

"Why?" Darcy said. "I mean, what in particular is she doing that's so awful?"

"Well, last week she told you that you had too much lipstick on. That just teed me off."

"She's a mother," Darcy said, smoothing his hair down. "They do that."

"Oh, yeah?" Stan said with challenge in his voice. "Do they also leave notes on the toilet telling you to put the seat down?"

"Fine," Darcy said, getting tired of this line of conversation. "We'll move in with your dad."

"Arrgh," Stan moaned.

"Shhhhh!" Darcy said and covered his mouth with

her hand. When she took it off, he was grouchier than ever.

"Great," he said. "We can't even talk."

"We can talk. Just don't make that noise. It sounds like we're . . ."

"Making love? Eeeek!" Stan made fun of her. "How could we even think of it? It's not like we're married or anything."

"Stan." She just wished he'd stop this and be quiet. But he'd found a way to tease her, and he wasn't about to stop. He was only getting started.

"Oh, my darling!" he shouted in the direction of the bedroom door. "Oh, honey, come here and give me a big kiss!"

"Stan! Shut up!" she said, but this only incited him to greater heights. He started jumping up and down on the bed, making the springs squeak, and then started making juicy kissing noises. If her mother was anywhere in earshot, Darcy knew what she must be thinking. She was so embarrassed she could die.

"Stan! You're going to break the bed!" she shouted. "Stop it!"

Then she realized that this made it sound even worse. She hoped her mother was down in the basement doing the laundry. No such luck. Just as Stan was winding up his Academy Award–winning performance, the bedroom door—apparently leaned against a little too hard—flew open and Mrs. Elliot stumbled into the room.

"Oh, excuse me," she said feebly. "I was just polishing the doorknobs and . . ." She backed out, blushing.

Darcy turned on Stan, furious at him for embarrassing her. "I'm going in to sleep with my mother," she told him.

"Fine," he said and started to get dressed.

"Just where are you going?" she asked him in a voice she didn't like hearing coming out of herself. The nagging wife.

"Same place I always go—out," Stan said. He was beginning to sound like the kind of husband who creates a naging wife—irresponsible, secretive, disappearing. Whenever trouble came up, he just left—always for the generic "out." Darcy never really knew where he went. She wasn't sure she wanted to.

That night, his first stop was the supermarket for a couple of six-packs. He was wheeling the cart slowly through the aisles—he liked the white light and bright colors of the supermarket, especially at night—tossing in anything that looked good. Taco chips, gum, a magazine.

When he was paying up, the checkout kid said, "Excuse me, sir. The lady wants to buy you a box of Pampers."

"Pardon?" Stan said, bewildered.

The checkout kid, every bit as confused as Stan, pointed down a few registers, and there was Michaela, holding up a huge box of disposable diapers.

"Very funny," he shouted sarcastically over to her, but he had to admit that it was, and they both looked at each other and started laughing.

"Want to take me for a ride?" he asked her as they walked out of the store together, pretty sure what her answer would be.

They parked out on the old country line road—"Make-Out Road," as it was called around Kenosha High. Stan opened a beer, and the foam sprayed all over both of them.

"Drink much?" Michaela ribbed him. They both

laughed at the same time, then fell into a slightly awkward silence.

"So . . . everybody's heading out for college next week, eh?" he said.

"Hey, it's okay," Michaela said. "You don't have to make conversation."

He knew she meant it, and he felt a huge wave of relief. Michaela reached into the bag of chips on the seat between them and took one and started nibbling on it. Stan watched her in silence.

"I think somebody just needs to hold you," she said to him now, in a *very* soft voice. "I don't think you need to talk or explain anything . . . or worry about what bills you're going to be able to pay."

She shifted a little, closing the distance between them. Stan didn't do anything to resist. With everything he'd been through lately, Michaela was probably right. He just needed somebody to not hassle him.

"You're a kid, Stan," Michaela went on, her voice low and soothing, like a hypnotist's. "I think you forgot that for a while. What Darcy did to you was lame. Really lame."

He opened another beer and took a long pull on it as he slid down in the seat. Then, still looking straight ahead through the windshield, he said, "You know how long I've been listening to my dad rave on about Cal Tech? Since I was ten years old."

He looked over at her and laughed. She laughed back appreciatively.

"I even learned their stupid fight song," he said, then paused for a while before telling her, "You'll never know what it felt like when I got the scholarship."

Michaela absorbed this information for a moment, then snapped, "And she talked you out of *that?*"

"She never knew I got it," Stan said. "But you

know what? When all the stuff went down . . . getting married . . . the baby . . . all of it . . ." He had to stop for a second, he felt himself getting choked up. He looked over at Michaela and told it to her straight. "I found out the feelings I had for Darcy were stronger than I could have had . . . for just about anything."

He looked Michaela in the eye, which wasn't too hard as her face was only inches from his.

"Get it straight, Michaela. That's not lame. That's love."

Having said this, there didn't seem to be anything else to say. So he just reached into the back seat for his bag of groceries and got out of the car. He shut the car door gently behind him as he left Michaela out on Make-Out Road—by herself.

Chapter 23

The worst thing about Darcy's job at the Pork Pit—worse than having to say, "May this little piggy help you?", worse than the smell of pork rinds sizzling in deep fat when they opened up the place at ten-thirty—was the hat she had to wear. It was basically a pair of paper pig ears. When she went to the washroom and passed the mirror, she died every time she saw how stupid she looked in it.

The hat had become symbolic of the job and all the things she hated about it. Her attitude was beginning to show. Today she was surlier than usual even and practically snarled her routine at the customers in line.

"Welcome to Pork Pit," she said, in about the same voice the devil would say, "Welcome to Hell."

"Two slabs of baby-back ribs and an order of rinds," the man said. He was fat. Almost all the customers at the Pork Pit were fat.

"Two cages and a side o' skins!" Darcy shouted into the microphone in front of her. There was a stupid lingo they were supposed to use in calling out the orders—another disgusting thing about the job.

"You're a cute little piggly wiggly," the guy said—his idea of flirting.

Darcy handed him his order number along with a look that said, "Don't even try."

She was so busy putting together his order that she

didn't notice until she got back to the mike just who her next customer was. Michaela. Probably here to make fun of her hat.

"Hi, Darcy. Or should I say, Oink Oink," she said with a smirk. "I had a couple of beers with Stan the other night. He didn't mention you were learning a new trade."

"Ribs or rinds, Michaela?" Darcy said. She'd had it with her hassling and her cheap jokes. And her determination to get Stan. Apparently she was having some success. He'd seen her at least one of those night he was "out."

"Don't worry," Michaela said, as though reading Darcy's mind. "Nothing happened. But he did mention how excited he was when he found out he was accepted at Cal Tech."

"You are so full of it," Darcy said, ignoring a glare from Ed Fitzsimmons, the assistant manager, who took the Pork Pit very seriously. Telling customers they were full of it was not what a good little piggy did.

"*Of course* he got in." Michaela was taunting Darcy now. "He just lied to you so he wouldn't break your little heart. How could you believe he didn't get in? He was an A student."

Darcy didn't know what to say to this—but Michaela did.

"I guess you believed it because you had to, eh, Darce?"

Darcy looked at Michaela, then at Ed Fitzsimmons, then at the long line of large customers growing irritable and impatient for ribs and rinds. Then she took off her pig ears, reached across the counter, gently smooshed them onto Michaela's head, and left.

* * *

She went straight to Chris's house. If anyone knew anything about Stan, it would be him.

He was out in his garage, rebuilding the transmission of his impossibly old car.

"What do you know about Stan getting into Cal Tech, getting that scholarship?"

"He didn't get it."

"That's what I thought, too," she told him, then relayed what Michaela had said. "Do you think it's true?" she asked him.

He thought for a moment, wiped his grease-blackened hands on his jeans, and said, "Could be. If he *did* get in, he wouldn't have told you. And he probably wouldn't have told me because he'd know you'd probably come around here one day asking. And he knew that if I knew, you'd worm it out of me."

Darcy had to smile. "So, how do we find out?"

Chris shrugged. "Make a few calls. Impersonate a couple of parents, a few teachers, maybe a principal. Can you do a decent Ms. Giles impersonation?"

Two hours down in Chris's basement, one notepad, and a six-pack of Cokes later, he and Darcy had finally gotten through the bureaucratic maze of higher education, and on the line with someone who could give them the information they wanted.

"Uh-huh," Darcy said. "Bobrucz, right? Uh-huh." She exhaled in relief and smiled at Chris. "So his scholarship *is* good. He can still go?"

She popped a pacifier into Thea's mouth and told the person on the other end, "Okay, okay. Great. And go ahead and—how did you put it? Yeah, that's it—'green light' him."

When she hung up, Chris said, "That's it?"

"That's it. Somebody canceled." She was a little

dumbfounded that with a few well-placed phone calls, she'd been able to change the course of Stan's immediate future.

"You thinking of going with him?" Chris asked.

"There's no married housing for undergrads," Darcy said, relaying the information she'd just gotten. "He has to live in a dorm and put in thirty hours a week work-study. With no income, it just wouldn't work out. I guess that's why he never told me."

"So what are you and Thea going to do?"

"Oh, we'll be okay," she said, putting on her brave voice.

"But what about *your* future?" he pressed. "What about Madison and journalism and—"

"I'll worry about that, okay?" Darcy snapped. "You just make sure he's on that plane next Thursday."

"But Darcy..."

"Look," she said. "They write bad country songs about this stuff, okay? The guy gets tied down too young. He starts hating the wife...the kid... everybody. And he ends up leaving anyway. This way, Stan leaves while there's still something to leave *for*."

The next afternoon, she was pacing around in her mother's kitchen. She'd been waiting for Stan since she got back from Chris's yesterday. A lot of nights now, Stan simply didn't come home, and when he finally did, there wasn't any explanation of where he'd been. It had become a point of pride with Darcy not to ask. Communication between the two of them had fallen to an all-time low.

She knew he had come to view her and the baby as stones around his neck, keeping him from flying free and soaring off into his future. It wasn't fair. The baby was holding *her* back from college, too—but she didn't look at Stan with silent resentment in her eyes. She had to admit, though, that one of them should probably have the chance to fly free of this. Stan had the scholarship. It should be him. The only question was how to get him to go. She'd have to be cold as ice. She'd have to convince him that she *wanted* him to go.

Finally she heard the front door slam. She stood still in the kitchen and waited until he came through the door. He looked so scruffy and haggard, his expression vacant. She could hardly see anymore the boy she'd fallen in love with.

"Sorry I didn't come home last night," he said, idly opening the refrigerator door to see what there was to eat.

Darcy took a deep breath and then dove into her plan. She'd had all night and most of the day to rehearse what she was going to say. She was ready.

"You have to go, Stan," she said firmly.

Stan turned around, looking bewildered, holding a carton of milk.

"Where?" he asked.

"Go. Leave. You've got to move out." She tried to keep her voice crisp and businesslike, not to let it break with any emotion.

Stan looked at her like he hadn't heard right.

"I'll apologize to your mother," he said quickly, trying to guess what she wanted.

"Forget my mother," Darcy said. "I'm talking about us. I'm not happy. You're not happy. You don't come home. And when you *do* come home . . ."

He picked up one of Thea's tiny T-shirts and began folding it. Darcy snatched it back. He wasn't making this easy.

"We'll work it out, Darcy," he said. "There's just a lot of . . . stuff now. We said once . . . that we could have it all . . ."

She couldn't let him go sentimental on her. Her plan required keeping this brisk and free of emotion.

"I want out, okay? I want a divorce."

"Divorce?" he said, as if she had reached out and slapped him. "We just got married—and not even very married."

"Fine," she said. "I'll get it annulled."

"Honey," he said, trying to put an arm around her, "you're just tired."

She hadn't wanted to raise her voice, but it looked like that was what it was going to take.

"I say get out!" she shouted. "Just do it. Just go through the door and—"

"No!" he shouted back.

"It's my house," Darcy said, pulling her trump card. "This is my house. Get out of it!"

But he wouldn't move. He just stood there, looking at her with wild pain in his eyes. She didn't know how she could make him move. She felt completely frustrated. The only thing she could think of to do was run out herself.

Stan stood in the kitchen alone for a moment, stunned. Then he ran after her. But Darcy was already out of the house. In the living room, he got stopped cold in his tracks when he saw Mrs. Elliot sitting calmly on the sofa, holding Thea. She gave him a cool look that distinctly said, "Don't you see you're not wanted around here? Why don't you be a nice boy and just leave?"

Chapter 24

Stan was sprawled across the pool table in Chris's family room. He had two days' worth of stubble on his face and was wearing the same clothes as when he'd left Darcy's. During those two days, he'd drunk a lot of beer. A tower of empty cans was precariously balanced on the edge of the pool table next to him. As he leaned over to top the pyramid with a final can, the entire structure came crashing down around him.

"I knew it," he said in a self-pitying voice. "I would have made a lousy architect."

Chris was working up to his speech, the one Darcy wanted him to give Stan. He was really uncomfortable with lying to his best friend, but he knew Darcy was probably right—Stan should go to Cal Tech and take the scholarship. And this was probably the only way to get him to go. He started, trying to sound casual and off-hand.

"Hey, look Stan. Maybe you should just can this family stuff. You know, get on with what you're supposed to be doing with your own life."

Stan laughed hollowly.

"You act like it's a course I'm taking. 'Marriage and the family.' Like I should just file a Drop Card and take something else. Get real."

"Listen," Chris said, "I called Cal Tech. Your scholarship's still good."

Stan looked at Chris as if he'd heard wrong.

"What?" he said, sitting up slowly, holding his head.

"Somebody canceled. They'll readmit you. We leave next Thursday."

Stan looked more confused than ever. He slid down off the table and began pacing around the room.

"Damn it! What are you doing, anyway? You're my friend. You're supposed to help me. I have enough problems without one more person running my life . . ." He got stopped midsentence by the sad look on Chris's face. He clapped a hand on his friend's shoulder and said, "I'm sorry, man. I mean, thanks. That must have taken some legwork."

"It was nothing. A few phone calls."

Stan had to smile. "I know. Just talking to about a million people."

Chris shrugged, making Stan think he was just being modest. He couldn't tell him that Darcy had made all the calls. She had sworn him to secrecy.

"Does Darcy know?" Stan asked suddenly, as though reading Chris's mind. And Chris almost told him, hesitating a second, wondering if he should, but then—sticking to his promise—he shook his head no.

"I appreciate it, okay?" Stan said. "No matter what I do. Anybody who'd go to that kind of trouble for me . . ." He put his arm around his friend. "That's somebody special."

Chris smiled limply, trapped uncomfortably in his lie. Upstairs, the doorbell rang. Chris's mother shouted down, "Chris, there's somebody up here to see Stan."

"Darcy?" Stan wondered to himself. He put down his beer and bolted upstairs and through the living room, out onto the front porch. There, waiting for him was, not Darcy, but a uniformed official. Stan came out, shielding his eyes from the sun. It had been a while since he'd seen actual daylight.

"Stanley Michael Bobrooz?" the man said.

"Bobrucz," Stan corrected him. What was this?

The man handed him an official-looking envelope and said, as though he'd said it a million times before, "I have been authorized by the State of Wisconsin to serve you with annulment papers."

Having slapped the envelope into Stan's hand, he turned and walked swiftly back down the walk. Stan —in shock—stared at the papers briefly, then ran after the guy, trying to give them back.

"Here! I don't want these! Take them back!" he shouted.

But the man was already getting into his car. Stan dropped the sheaf of papers and then hurriedly tried to pick them up, but the guy had already started his car and was driving off. Stan stood in the middle of the street, holding the papers aloft, yelling at the back of the car, "Yeah, well that's great, buddy! Only one problem. We were never married!"

Behind him, Chris watched Stan and winced, comprehending his friend's pain.

That night, Stan showed up at Darcy's house clutching the torn annulment papers. He rang the doorbell, then when there was no answer rang it again. Then again. He kept leaning on it off and on for a long time. Darcy and her mother sat inside, in the dark, pretending they weren't home. Darcy could tell from the way Stan was raving that he'd been drinking again. He sounded completely out of control.

"Darcy! Darcy!" he shouted. "I just want to talk to

you. These papers are wrong. They say we were never married. We *were* married! We have a *baby!* Did you forget? *I* didn't forget. Because I love you. And you loved me. And . . . we had a home . . . and a kid . . . some problems, sure . . . but so much feeling for each other. Oh Darcy, *please* . . ."

She was about ready to give in and open the door to him. He sounded so pitiful. She turned to her mother, who was sitting next to her on the sofa, and was about to ask her if maybe they shouldn't relent and let him in, when Mrs. Elliot looked at her watch and said, "That's twenty minutes. I'm calling the police." She got up and started for the phone.

"Mom . . . don't," Darcy said softly. As she was saying it, the buzzing stopped. She closed her eyes, relieved.

"He needs to go for counseling," her mother said.

At this point, the doorbell buzzing was replaced by the loud beeping of the horn on Chris's truck.

Darcy's mother shot her an "I told you so" look and started for the phone again.

"It's called 'tough love,' Darcy."

Darcy got up from the couch, worried.

"They might put him in jail," she told her mother. "If they do, will he be out by Thursday? He has to go . . . to school."

Clearly this wasn't her mother's main concern. She just kept heading for the phone, picking it up and then punching out 911.

The next morning, Stan woke up feeling like someone had wedged an axe between his eyes, and like a small furry creature was nesting in his mouth. The worst hangover of his life so far. He opened his eyes slowly and looked around. At first he thought Chris's basement was just a more depressing dump than he remembered. Then he saw the bars.

"Oh, boy," he said out loud.

About an hour later, a policeman opened the door to the cell. "You can go now. Your old man's here to take you home."

Stan could see his father waiting at the end of the long, dark hallway. When he got to him, they stood for a moment in awkward silence before Mr. Bobrucz said, "Some friends you've got. They shouldn't never have let you get drunk like that."

"Did it all by myself," Stan said, smart-alecky. They were both trying for the familiar rough-edged, sarcastic tone they used with each other, but neither of them could quite find it today, or really had the heart to. Mr. Bobrucz pushed the heavy metal door open for Stan, and they walked together out of the police station.

"Look," Stan's dad said as they walked, "I go bowling once a week. I drink three beers. I go home."

He walked ahead of Stan toward the parking lot and continued. "Some of the other guys—they get loaded. Stay out all night."

As he moved toward the car he turned and looked back at Stan and said, "So, what kind of dad are you going to be?"

Stan looked at him and nodded slightly to show he got the point, and they got in the car together. Father and son.

Later, Stan sat on his old bed—the one his dad hadn't let him take—surrounded by pamphlets and brochures and orientation-week schedules for Cal

Tech. His father stuck his head in the doorway, then knocked on the doorframe to let Stan know he was there.

"What are you going to do about Cal Tech?" he asked.

Stan shrugged, picked up a few of the pamphlets, then dropped them back on the bed, clearly lost.

"Got to decide by Thursday. Maybe I should go, eh? Chance of a lifetime."

"Still no word from Darcy?" Mr. Bobrucz asked.

Stan shook his head sadly.

"You really love her, don't you?"

"Aw, Dad. When I try to see the rest of my life without her . . . I can't even breathe."

Stan's father looked at him with love, then fumbled for a moment, trying to find the right words.

"Look, I know I've always been pushing you to be somebody—somebody I wasn't . . ."

Stan could see this was really hard for him. It showed all over his father's face. And so he didn't interrupt, just waited until his dad finished, saying, "Just make damn sure whatever you do—you do it for you, not for *me*."

And then he did something he hadn't done since Stan was about five—walked over and gave him a big, bearlike hug.

Chapter 25

The graduation at Kenosha Night School was a low-key affair. There were no caps or gowns, no big speeches, no organ playing "Pomp and Circumstance." The twenty or so graduates received their diplomas to small bursts of applause from their friends and relatives. Darcy got a round of clapping from her mother and Ms. Giles, and sharp little squealing and gurgling sounds from Thea.

After the brief ceremony, everyone gathered around the punch bowl and toasted one another with apple juice in paper cups.

Ms. Giles lifted hers and said, "To Darcy Elliot-Bobrucz, who did the right thing, who saw the mountain and . . ."

". . . and walked right through it," an embarrassed Darcy said, making everyone laugh.

Mrs. Elliot, who was playing with Thea, dangled her car keys in front of the baby's grabbing little hands.

"And this is just the beginning for you, honey," she said to Darcy. "And for Thea. You both have to reach for what's out there, beyond your grasp."

Darcy wished she could just leave before anyone else embarrassed her. No such luck. From across the room, suddenly, there was Stan—bounding toward her, shouting, stopping pretty much all conversation in the room.

"Darcy!"

"Come on," Darcy's mother said to her. "I don't want a scene." She turned to Ms. Giles and said good-bye. Darcy, too.

"Bye," she told the guidance counselor. "And thanks."

Ms. Giles just stood there looking confused.

"It's a long story," Darcy said as she let her mother pull her out of the room with Stan running after them, still shouting like a madman, "Darcy! Darcy!"

They ducked out a side door, but he spotted them and chased them into the parking lot.

"Darcy, wait up! I've got to talk to you!"

Darcy and her mother rushed to get into the car and shut the doors.

"Wait, please," Stan said, pressing his hands against the windows.

"Hands off the car," Mrs. Elliot said coldly, raising her power window the last inch or two as Stan quickly pulled his fingers out of the way. Then he started pulling at the door handle.

"Come on, Mrs. Elliot. Give me a break."

Her answer to this was to pull the car out of its space and into the line moving out of the lot. He started jogging next to the car. Mrs. Elliot rolled down her window halfway and tried to dispatch him with reason.

"Look, Stan. You're a good kid. You tried your best. But if you really love Darcy, give her a chance. I can help her make something of herself . . ."

"She was doing okay by herself, Mrs. Elliot. That made you nervous, didn't it?" He ran around to Darcy's side of the car.

She shouted out to him, "Stan. Don't do this. Please. We gave it our best shot. We just couldn't cut it. That's all." She tried to make it sound simple and clearcut, as though there really wasn't anything more to discuss. Thursday was only two days away, and she wanted him to have that scholarship. She had to keep up her front of wanting to get rid of him. It was the only way to get him to go.

"Hey, I love you," he shouted in the window now. He was not making this easy. "I'll never stop loving you. Thea . . . tell your mother . . ."

But Thea was rolling into a full-tilt crying jag, screaming at the top of her lungs, drowning out Stan's pleas, and absorbing all of Darcy's attention for the moment. But not even this stopped Stan. Still running alongside the car, he told Darcy, "I went to Madison today. I put in for scholarships. Journalism —*and* the School of Architecture. And I gave your article—about having the baby—to Markus. He—"

"You gave my *what?*" Darcy said, horrified.

"He loved it. He wrote you a letter. He wants to publish it in the paper. Here . . ." he said, sliding the letter through the open crack in the window.

"And these are for you, too," he said, signaling for her to put down the window so he could hand her a bouquet of flowers. "There's something inside." Then he gave her a little box. "For Thea," he said.

Darcy was getting upset. She didn't want Stan trying to make up with her. It just made it harder to be cold to him, and she had to keep up the freeze-out if she was going to get him on that plane to California.

"Cut it out!" she shouted out the window. "Just stop it!"

But he was already pushing more stuff through the opening in the window. Literature this time.

"Here's some stuff on married housing and child-care co-ops." He looked at Thea. "See, she stopped crying. She likes the sound of it."

"Look. Go to California, Stan," Darcy finally

blurted out. "They're holding your place. Don't blow your dream!"

"Holding my place?" Stan said, "How did you know?" And then everything became clear to him. It showed on his face. "Is that why you kicked me out?"

But Mrs. Elliot was getting close to the street now, and the cars were speeding up. He had to jump out of the way or get run over. He risked it to shout into the car. "You still love me, don't you Darcy? Darcy . . . do you still love me?"

Inside the car, Darcy started sobbing, but Stan didn't see it because Mrs. Elliot had already pulled into the street and immediately sped up. Stan ran after the car until it turned a corner, then stood in the middle of the street shouting into the night, "Daaarrrcccy!!!"

Darcy fought back tears as she held Thea tight, trying to think while her mother attempted to smooth things over.

"He would have just left you someday," she was saying.

Darcy sat in silence, watching Stan get smaller and smaller in the sideview mirror.

"We have each other, honey," her mother went on —making her crazy. Oblivious to this, Mrs. Elliot went on. "Remember when Daddy left us? You filled a big space in my life. Now it's my turn to do the same for you."

These words sank in. Darcy thought about what her mother was saying. "Not everybody's daddy leaves, Mother," she told her.

"Sooner or later, everybody leaves," Mrs. Elliot said.

"No, you're wrong," Darcy said, confronting her mother with what she knew to be the truth. "Love is about . . . sticking around. Stan got into Cal Tech, but he didn't go. Because he cares about me and Thea. He . . . he doesn't take a hike the minute something goes wrong." She thought about this for a minute, then came up with another truth. "Like I do."

All of a sudden, Darcy's head filled with a million images of her and Stan, all the past they shared, and all the days to come. No matter how rocky they might be, she couldn't imagine living them without him. She turned toward her mother.

"Stop the car right now. Pull over."

Amazingly, her mother didn't fight her, didn't say anything, just pulled to a stop at the curb. With Thea in her arms, Darcy got out and looked in through the open window.

"Look, Mom. You've got a choice to make, okay? You either love all of us . . . or none of us." Darcy could tell that her mother was a little taken aback by these words, but when she finally responded, it was to say, "Here, honey. You'd better take my sweater. It might get chilly later."

Darcy nodded. She knew this was her mother's way of saying it was okay, that Darcy would have to do what she had to do.

"Thanks," Darcy said, nodding toward the sweater, but really meaning a whole lot more. She used the sweater to bundle up Thea. Holding the baby to her chest, she looked in once more at her mother, then turned and started down the dark street, back to the night school.

A few minutes later, Mrs. Elliot pulled up in front of her house, followed by the sound of screeching brakes. She turned to see Stan leaning out the window of his car.

"Where's Darcy?"

She looked back at him for a long moment, not saying anything.

"Could you give me a hint?" he asked sarcastically.

Mrs. Elliot took a long time before she answered. "She went . . . looking for you. Back to the school."

Stan ground the gearshift into first and started off down the street. Then he jammed on the brakes, threw the car into reverse, and backed up to the house. He looked sincerely at Mrs. Elliot and said, this time without a trace of sarcasm in his voice, "Thanks."

She wasn't used to this tone from Stan and was a little nonplussed. She waved him off with a slight smile. He nodded and headed off to find Darcy . . .

. . . who, at the moment, was sitting on a bench in the night school's playground, sniffling and talking to her daughter.

"I guess we really blew it this time, didn't we, Thea? Come on. Let's get you home." She got up and started walking dejectedly toward the street. Suddenly, Stan drove into the parking lot behind her, got out of the car, and began shouting, "Darcy! Darcy!"

She turned and watched him run toward her and the baby. All of a sudden they were overlapping each other with the huge tumble of their emotions.

"Oh, Stan, I'm sorry. I never meant to . . ."

"Cal Tech doesn't mean anything. Forget Cal Tech. You and Thea mean everything to me."

"But that's all you ever talked about . . . all you ever wanted."

"I want you. I want Thea."

"Okay," Darcy said, "but what about my mother?"

"It's okay," he said. "We talked."

"Okay. But what about money? We still don't have any."

"We'll sell the car."

"Okay, but what about . . ."

Instead of letting her finish, Stan put his hands on her shoulders and kissed her.

"Did you look in the flowers?" he said, reaching inside the bouquet she was still holding onto. He came out with a small velvet ring box, opened it, and handed her a real gold band.

"This one doesn't bend," he said, looking shyly into Darcy's eyes. "You see, I was hoping maybe you'd want to marry me."

Darcy paused for a second, then raised an eyebrow and teased him. "Marry you? Do you know what the odds are against teenage marriages?"

Stan nodded and smiled and said, "We can beat 'em."

"Then I guess you've got yourself a wife," Darcy said.

They stood in the middle of the playground—an oddly appropriate setting for the end of their childhood, the beginning of Thea's—and embraced.

"We'd better get Thea home," Darcy said. "It's way past her bedtime."

As they started walking back to the car, Stan said, "When this kid's a teenager, she's gonna have a curfew."

"Definitely," Darcy agreed.

"Ten o'clock," Stan said.

"Well," Darcy said, looking down at Thea, "maybe eleven o'clock, if they're really in love."

"If they're really in love—eight o'clock," Stan said and smiled and stopped and kissed her.

"I love you, Darcy."

"I love you too, Stan," she said.

They looked at each other and got into the car and sputtered off, into the night, and into their future.